NOVICE MYSTERY
ITALY

THE FOURTH DAN & KAREN NOVICE MYSTERY

DONNA REWOLINSKI

www.ten16press.com - Wauwatosa, WI

I'd like to thank my husband, Frank, for his love, support, and technical advice. Also, I want to thank Kim Suhr and members of the Thursday night Red Oak Writing critique group, who have read, edited, reread, and provided guidance through the publishing process.

A very special thanks to James Hass of Old Dog Design for his willingness to provide ideas for my book covers. His willingness to lend his talent to my books was appreciated and touching beyond words.

CHAPTER 1

The plane lands at the Venice Marco Polo Airport. I can't believe we're here. *Italy.* Yeah. Another trip. The first since our disaster of a vacation to France over a year and a half ago. A shiver runs through me when I think back to our involvement with the murder mystery weekend that was more like Agatha Christie's *And Then There Were None* meets *Clue*. I recall the message from my friend, Honoré, that informed us that Monsieur Bres passed away a few weeks after the inquest that involved all of us. A wave of sadness washes over me. I hope to see our friends again during happier times. What are we doing traveling again? Our last three vacations have involved ten dead bodies, multiple investigations, crime scene evidence work, not to mention my wife, Karen, solving most of the murders.

Karen is the love of my life. Shoulder-length reddish-brown hair, hazel eyes, and an innate ability to read people. She looks around the airport as we make our way through customs and claim our luggage. Her eyes tell me she's happy to be here. I need to relax and not be an impediment to her enjoying this trip.

Lorenzo said that he couldn't be at the airport but sent a

boat driver to pick us up and take us to a restaurant near San Marco where he'll meet us after a mandatory work meeting. Lorenzo Conte is a crime reporter in Venice. Several years ago, I contacted him after I read an intriguing article he had written. It had been translated from Italian to English and posted on an investigator's website. We've continued to correspond.

I take Karen's hand as we exit the airport. We find a man holding a sign with our last name.

"*Il Signore e Signora* Novice, *sì?*" he asks. He's in his early thirties, with deep dark-brown hair, eyes that match, and lean, tanned muscle.

"Yes, I'm Dan, and this is my wife, Karen." I extend my hand to him. His handshake is firm and dry.

"I am Marco Bruni. Please follow me. My boat is waiting."

He takes Karen's luggage. I follow behind. We step out to a royal blue sky. Boats buzz up and down the waterway. Marco leads us to a high-gloss mahogany wood boat with antique brass accents. He steps in and assists Karen, then me. The bench seats, each covered in a deep red leather, form a giant U at the back of the boat. Once we're situated, Marco steps up to the wheel and starts the engine. The boat sways gently as it cuts through the water with ease. The scents of fish and salt reach my nose.

Marco's head pivots from side to side, scanning all around him. Karen nestles into me. I know she's happy to be here, and to be truthful, so am I. We look around us. Buildings majestically rise out of the turquoise waters. Stone edifices colored cream, tangerine, tan, and rose blend Eastern and Western architecture. Byzantine tiles, Moroccan-styled windows, and large arched doorways grace the front of the structures. Red and orange terracotta roof tiles punctuate the deep blue sky. Balconies look down on this site, beckoning visitors to come and stay. Narrow waterways weave from the Grand Canal and under medieval bridges like arteries to connect neighborhoods to the heart of the city. Moored boats of all sizes bob with the rhythm of the water.

Boats navigate the canals in number and speed. *This must be rush hour Venetian-style.* What appears as pure chaos seems to flow as we approach the center of Venice. The walkways are jammed with people, some in costumes and masks, some without. Street performers entertain pedestrians. Karen smiles broadly as she points to various sights, but I can't hear anything she says over the sound of the motor.

Marco aligns the boat to a small dock and secures a line at both the front and back of the vehicle. Karen and I step onto the pier while Marco speaks to two young men who collect our luggage.

"They come from the villa," Marco says. "They will make sure everything gets to your room."

I'm uneasy with that but know that Karen and I have retained our passports, credit cards, and cash. Worst-case scenario, we buy new clothes.

Marco motions for us to follow him. "Lorenzo will meet us at the *ristorante*, Il Sogno, *sì*?" He doesn't wait for a reply, but rather starts to move along the walkway that hugs the canal. Karen and I struggle to keep up given the crowds of people in all directions. I try to calm myself as it bothers me to be surrounded by so many masked people. Music, laughter, and a variety of spoken languages punctuate the air while aromas of eateries, bakeries, and coffee shops drift out of doorways as we pass. Marco stops at a small storefront with a centered doorway, the windows to each side decorated with red-and-white checkerboard curtains. Across from it is a platform that extends from the walkway over a portion of the canal. Tables with white linen tablecloths adorn the terrace, and a yellow canvas canopy provides cover from the day's sun. Marco heads inside and returns with a tall, thin man with sharp, rat-like features, black hair, and a barely there moustache. The man's face lights up as he wipes his hands on his apron before extending one to me. "Welcome to my place. I am Andrea Sarto."

I shake his hand, which is warm and moist, but firm. Marco waves as he heads back toward his boat.

"Come. Sit." Andrea picks up two menus and directs me and Karen to a table with a view of the canal. "Lorenzo will come soon." He places a menu in front of each of us. "What would you like to drink? Some wine, maybe?"

"I'd like some sparkling water," Karen says.

I order a large Italian beer. Andrea scribbles on his pad with a nod before returning inside the restaurant.

Karen swivels in her chair, taking in the people and their costumes. Slowly the place fills up until there are no empty tables. It's a visual masterpiece. An unreal land filled with elaborate fantasy creatures. Everyone different from each other. Costume and mask colors both sublime and bold. Feathers, jewels, and glitter in abundance.

She reaches across the table and rubs the top of my hand as we study the menu. "I want us to have the best time here.

Venice during Carnival with someone who knows the area. I'm sure it'll be amazing."

Andrea reappears, setting our drinks in front of us. "What would you like to eat?" he asks.

Karen orders spaghetti carbonara. I choose to start with an appetizer of mussels and clams, then for dinner spaghetti with fruits of the sea. I'm not quite sure what that means, but I'm in Venice, known for its seafood.

I self-talk that the Carnival participants are having innocent fun, but my "coppy senses" are elevated. I force a deep, calming breath and repeat to myself, *I'm on vacation.*

"It's like a living, moving rainbow," Karen says. "The costumes, masks, headdresses, and decorations in every color, texture, and design. I can't decide which I like best."

I notice one person, dressed in all black: shirt, pants, cloak, hat, and a bizarre long-beaked mask. I point to them.

"The plague doctor," Karen replies.

"Plague doctor?"

"Yeah, the outfit was developed to protect doctors while treating patients during the bubonic plague in Europe. It was thought that the long beak protected the doctors. It was filled with herbs that were to filter and purify the air the doctor was breathing in."

"Wow, that must have been a horrible sight to see."

"They're creepy-looking, but we'll see quite a few this week," Karen states.

The word "sinister" pops into my head. I shiver at the unsettling outfit.

Andrea is back with the appetizer. The huge mussels and

clams swim in a rich white sauce, and the aroma reminds me I haven't eaten in hours.

My first bite is delicious. "Perfect," I tell Andrea.

He beams back at me. *Buon appetito.*"

I finish off the last of it as Andrea delivers our dinners. Karen takes the first forkful and hums quietly with satisfaction. "This is amazing. The best I've ever eaten."

I tuck into mine and agree with her assessment. Forkfuls are periodically interrupted by people watching and enjoying the upbeat jazz music that seems to emanate from all around us. We are scraping the last morsels from our plates when a man approaches our table. I recognize those dark, penetrating eyes, large nose, and eyebrows that seem to grow together. It's Lorenzo. I stand up to shake his hand.

"Ahhh, Daniel. *Benvenuto.* This must be your lovely wife," Lorenzo says as he makes eye contact with Karen. I've only ever seen him on my computer screen, and he's taller than I imagined. He plops into a chair next to me. Andrea pours him a large glass of red wine.

Lorenzo swishes the contents of the glass. "I eat here three or four times a week. They know what I like. How was your dinner?"

"Delicious," Karen replies happily. "Are you going to eat? We're in no hurry."

He shakes his head. "No, we had food at the meeting. Dinner in Italy is to be savored."

"I need to pay for our meal," I state.

Lorenzo dismisses me with a wave of his hand. "No, Andrea is just happy you like your dinner."

My eyes dart to Andrea, who avoids my eye contact for a moment, then hurries back to the kitchen.

"I will, as you Americans say, 'treat you,'" Lorenzo says. "Andrea will bill me later." He leans back in his chair, sipping his wine.

Bewilderment looms as Karen shoots me a sideways glance. I shift uncomfortably in my chair. Does he pay, or is he just saying that and expects the owner to provide free meals? Lorenzo may indulge in a free meal, but I have never allowed myself to take advantage of my position when I was working, and I won't now. This is disconcerting for me. How well do I really know Lorenzo? I have an idea of what our bill would've been.

Lorenzo leans forward, placing his elbows on the table. "Two of the best private parties are held at the villa where you are staying. You are invited to both. Lord and Lady Ravenscraft have hosted a masquerade ball every year since they moved here many years ago. Old money." Once again, he reclines, taking another sip of wine. "You like my city so far?"

Karen looks around and smiles. "Absolutely magnificent."

Lorenzo nods and drains his glass, places the empty cup on the table, and stands up. "Ready?"

"This was amazing. Thank you," I say. "I'm going to personally tell Andrea how much we liked it, and I want a card from the restaurant so I can remember it when I get home."

Karen starts a conversation with Lorenzo as I catch up with Andrea. A handshake between us disguises my pressing money into his hand. He makes eye contact. I wink and turn to join Karen and Lorenzo as we begin to navigate the street toward where we're staying this week. Karen slips her hand in mine. This kind of vacation I can do.

"*Signora*, if you are not too tired, I would like to take you to your first fitting now, then your dress will be *perfetto* for the ball," Lorenzo says.

We saunter along the Grand Canal, dodging revelers, jugglers, mimes, and musicians. Luckily, I have hold of Karen's hand, as she's at risk of being swept away and possibly joining a new street performance group.

She rubs my arm. "Being here makes me so happy. It feels as if we're immersed in joy. I can't get enough. I want to stay and experience it all."

Lorenzo weaves his way among, around, and at times straight through the crowds. I work to remember the turns he makes and any street names. Hopefully he'll walk us to where we're staying, as I have no idea of how to get there. He stops in front of a light pink, two-story building. Bright costumes, masks, and shoes fill the display windows that flank the door. Lorenzo lets himself into the shop. The jingle of a brass bell alerts the staff we're here. The smells of warm fabric and a hint of garlic, possibly from lunch, reach my nose. I think of the welcoming, inviting feel of the store, when from behind the black velvet curtain at the back of the room comes a scream.

CHAPTER 2

A woman is standing against an inside wall of the shop, a frown on her face. She's twenty-something, small-boned, with a mousy brown bob haircut. Another young woman with dark brown, waist-length hair and even darker eyes steps out from behind the curtain. She's pointing to a back room, sobbing words in Italian.

I look to Lorenzo. "What's she saying?"

"That she is dead." His brow is furrowed.

"Who?" I demand.

"Her mother, Anna."

"Whose mother? What's going on?"

"This is Arielle Giudice. She helps her mother with the costumes. She says her mother is dead." He looks between me and Arielle.

I push past Lorenzo into the back room to find an elderly woman dressed in a black dress lying on her back on the floor. I feel her neck for a pulse, finding none. She is still warm to the touch.

Lorenzo hovers over me with his cell phone, speaking rapidly in Italian. I hope he's calling for emergency services and not a story to his newspaper. "*Polizia*," he says.

I survey the room. Fabrics, ribbons, pins, threads, feathers, and gems fill containers and every inch of the work surfaces. Remnants of each form a collage of colors and textures on the floor around the body. Curiously out of place is an overturned box about the size of a small jewelry case and pins scattered next to the body.

I stand up and direct Lorenzo back to the front of the shop. Arielle is sitting on a chair, swaying and sobbing into her cell phone. Karen has her arm around Arielle and looks up at me. I shake my head.

The other woman in the store says with a strong British accent, "Look, I'm just here to pick up my mother's gown. I don't know anything about what happened. Can I go?" She moves toward the door.

I step in front of the door to block her way. "No. Not until the police have had a chance to question each of us. What's your name?"

She throws up her hands with a dramatic sigh. "Katherine Oldman. I don't understand why I have to wait around. I said I don't know anything."

Minutes tick by. I review what my statement to the police will be, given what I'd observed, until I turn to see a figure with the build of a Roman gladiator coming through the door. Well, maybe a thin gladiator. He nods acknowledgement to Lorenzo. Behind him are two uniformed officers carrying crime scene equipment, who are directed to where the body is.

"*Buona sera.*" A mild baritone voice accompanies an oblong face with a ruddy complexion.

Arielle chokes out something. Lorenzo talks over her. I

look between them, hoping someone translates what is being said. The gladiator makes eye contact with me.

"I'm sorry, I don't speak Italian," I say.

"I am *Commissario* Vincenzo Caputo. I'm in charge. What has happened?"

Katherine steps forward. "I just came to pick up my mother's dress." She waves her finger in the direction of Arielle. "She went into the back room for a couple of minutes, then came out screaming and crying, all in Italian. I didn't know what was happening, then those other people came in."

Caputo's eyes flick to me. I introduce myself and Karen and explain why we're there, what I observed since arriving in the shop, and our alibi since arriving in Venice.

The *commissario* listens intently, his eyes never wavering. He nods periodically with his lips pressed together until I finish.

"You are police, *sì*." He says it more like a statement than a question.

I nod. "Retired. How did you know?"

A sly smile creeps across Caputo's lips. "The way you described the scene. Only one who has seen this before would be so calm and remember the details needed for the investigation."

A frown creases my forehead. "Do you think this is anything but a natural death?"

He shrugs. "Everyone stay here. My officers are securing the area, and I will need a statement from you each." Caputo moves to the back room. Katherine drops into a chair near Arielle.

Karen stands in front of me. She rolls her eyes.

"What? I'm not getting involved. I promise." I place my hand over my heart.

Time crawls along. Karen rubs Arielle's back. I feel the jet lag settling into my whole body. I start to pace in an attempt to stay awake while waiting to be formally interviewed. Finally, Caputo begins asking each person to step into a side room. Arielle is first. Moments later, she comes back, yelling at Katherine. Karen and I look at each other, then to Lorenzo.

"What's wrong?" Karen asks him.

"Arielle is saying that Katherine handed her a box, which she gave to her mother. Anna opened the box, saw the beautiful pins inside, and started using them. Anna hurt her finger, then had seizures and died. Arielle blames Katherine for her mother's death."

Katherine jumps to her feet and waves her hands at Arielle. "No, no, I found the box outside near the door. I just brought it inside. I don't know anything. You have to believe me." Katherine looks around the room for support or sympathy.

Karen and I exchange confused looks. How could a few pinpricks have caused the death?

Caputo is standing just outside the doorway, listening, then asks Katherine into the side room. After Katherine rejoins us, Lorenzo, Karen, and I are each interviewed. Caputo verifies all of our alibis and releases us after taking information for where we will be staying. Katherine looks through a rack of garments bags, then grabs one and hurries out of the shop.

Arielle looks at Karen. "You come tomorrow to try on your dress."

Karen shakes her head. "No, I'm sure my dress will be fine."

"No, *signora*, you must come tomorrow. I can do this for you."

Lorenzo opens the door. "The *polizia* say it is okay to leave. We will come tomorrow at ten in the morning. *Grazie*, Arielle. *Arrivederci*."

I guess we're leaving. Karen grabs both of Arielle's hands. "I'm so sorry for your loss."

I have my hand on the small of Karen's back as we start for the door. We're brushed back as a tall, dark-haired man pushes his way through the entrance. The man points to Arielle and angrily barks something in Italian. Arielle's eyes are studying the floor.

Karen looks at Lorenzo. "Who's that?"

"Her brother, Mario," he replies.

My question is, "Is it safe to leave her alone with him?"

"He is not nice, but she is safe. It is family business, not ours."

Mario's angry voice penetrates the air from the back room. I don't understand the words, but I do understand the emotion, and it sounds abusive. I grab Lorenzo's arm. "What's Mario saying?"

Lorenzo sighs. "He's angry that Arielle did not take his advice earlier. Their father left the business to their mother. Mario wanted her to sell, but Arielle supported their mother, who refused. He works in London and wants the money so his mother could retire."

Karen takes my hand. "I feel so sorry for Arielle. He could be kind to her today of all days."

Caputo appears from the back room and approaches Mario. Karen and I follow Lorenzo outside.

"Did Caputo say anything about what he thinks happened? Does he think Anna died of natural causes?" I ask.

Lorenzo waves his hand dismissively. "No, he did not say."

Karen sighs. "Do you think Arielle will need to sell the shop now that her mother is dead?"

"I do not know. It is Mario's decision. He knows what is best." Lorenzo walks rapidly in the direction of our bed-and-breakfast. Karen and I quicken our pace until he suddenly stops in front of a pharmacy.

"Please forgive me. I must go in here for my medication," he says, pulling the glass door open. Karen and I look at each quizzically.

The store is one big room. Glass-top cases circle most of the inside, and two center aisles display vitamins and various over-the-counter medications as well as other medical items. An older couple waits near the register.

Lorenzo shouts, "*Salve!*" several times. A young woman with shoulder-length, rich, brown, curly hair stands up from behind a counter.

"Ahh, Danielle, good you are here. I have my heart medication to pick up. Is it ready?" Lorenzo then points in our direction. "These are my friends, Dan *e* Karen Novice from America."

Danielle smiles in our direction. "*Sì*, your prescription is ready." Lorenzo pushes past the elderly people in line at the register. Danielle verbalizes something in Italian that I think may translate into "Wait your turn" as Lorenzo steps to one side. Danielle finishes the sale and bids the couple good night. Lorenzo pays for his medication, and we leave. Karen and I wave to Danielle on our way out.

Lorenzo is muttering, "Those two old people have been

talking to anyone they can about their seven-day bus tour to Rome." His tone is one of disgust. "I hope I am never so old that I need to repeat my stories again and again."

Karen rolls her eyes and stifles a laugh.

My "coppy senses" are heightened. There are far too many people moving in all directions around me, and pickpockets can be ever present. I walk as often as possible with a building to one side of myself and Karen slightly in front of me. The constant search for an easily defensible position. Lorenzo stops in front of a five-story home, painted a deep tangerine. A large double door of dark wood and metal rivets stands before us. The second- and third-story windows each sport a white stone balcony with six fluted balusters holding up the railing.

"We are here," Lorenzo announces.

Karen smiles. "It's beautiful."

"I am glad you like it, *signora*. It was built in the year 1483 by a member of the Medici family."

"Medici?" Karen questions. "I thought they were only in Florence."

"No, no, the family came here too. Venice liked the money they brought."

Lorenzo opens the door for us, and the smell of lavender enters our noses. The entrance hall is exquisite. Deep red, scalloped tiles cover the floor, seeming to point in the direction of a small wooden desk. Hand-hewed beams run across the ceiling with large crystal chandeliers hanging in between. Concrete pillars two stories tall rise on either side of the pink room. A petite elderly woman in a tailored grey pinstriped dress steps out from a side room to greet us.

"*Benvenuto*," she states with a warm smile. I guess her to be in her early seventies, her straight white hair cut in a neat bob. Her only accessory is a three-strand pearl choker; sagging neck skin peeks out below it.

Lorenzo steps forward. "Lady Ravenscraft, let me introduce *Signore e Signora* Dan and Karen Novice from America."

"So glad you've made it. Welcome to Casa de Inglese," she says with a strong British accent. "I was expecting you both *sooner*."

Muttering under my breath, I say, "We were planning on being here sooner."

"Please speak up. I just can't abide by men that mutter," Lady Ravenscraft snaps.

I press a smile on my lips. "We're glad to be here now."

Karen reaches out her hand. "Thank you so much, Lady Ravenscraft."

"Do call me Harriet, dear. Your room is ready. Your luggage arrived and has already been placed in it."

I sigh a breath of relief.

Harriet turns her clear, sky-blue eyes to me. "I'm sorry, your name again?"

"Dan," I say, extending my hand.

After the briefest of contacts, she releases my grip, then speaks as if addressing a class of children. "Breakfast is served promptly at 8:00 a.m. It's a full English breakfast with eggs, sausages, tomatoes, beans, toast, and coffee or tea. The expectation is that you either arrive on time or send word that you will not be coming. Wasted food is such a nuisance."

Karen and I are frozen in place after the stern instructions.

A portly man with a bad gray combover marches into the room, coughing, a smoking pipe in his hand.

"Arthur, put that silly pipe away," Harriet declares. He quickly places it in the right pocket of his tweed jacket. She continues, "I was about to say there is *NO* smoking inside. If you must smoke, please confine yourself to the street out front."

"Not a problem. Neither of us smoke," Karen replies.

"Arthur, come here," Harriet says. He quickly obeys, stands before Karen and me, and grabs my hand. "Lord Arthur Ravenscraft. Bloody good you're here, old chap, and you as well, my dear." Not sure if he's playing his assigned role or just glad his wife has someone else to focus on in the house.

Harriet pats his shoulder. "Yes, yes, Arthur, be off while I settle our guests."

The lord tut-tuts a few times and wanders back from where he came.

Harriet pulls a key from the top of the desk and turns toward a sweeping stone staircase. "Follow me."

Karen and I fall in line behind her. She calls over her shoulder as she climbs the stairs. "The maid comes in daily around 10:00 a.m. Nice girl. Bit flighty. Never on time, but a good worker. I call her Joanna, as she reminds me of my niece. Much the same personality. Can't remember what her given name is, but she answers to Joanna."

Karen turns to me with a "What the heck" look. I rub her back in acknowledgement. At the top of the stairs, Harriet makes a sharp left and walks toward the third door on the right, where she stops and uses the key. She pushes the door open and crosses into the room. We follow.

Soft blue, swirl-patterned wallpaper, thick drapes in the same color, and a king-size bed with a wrought iron frame catch my eye.

"It's wonderful," Karen tells Harriet.

She pats Karen's hand. "So glad you like it, my dear. Your bathroom is in there." She waves a bony finger in a general direction off to our left before turning back to Karen. "Here's your key. I'll provide further information regarding the activities in the manor later tonight. Enjoy." She retreats to the hallway, closing the door behind her.

Karen heads to the French doors and opens them. Curious, are they still called "French" doors if you're in Italy? I snort a laugh to myself in reply.

"Dan, come see. We have a view of the Grand Canal. This is everything I imagined a room in Venice should be." Karen rests her hands on the balcony's iron railing and turns toward me. "Minus finding a dead body on the first day."

I wrap my arms around her as we look out over the water. Upbeat music wafts up to us. The smells of warm tomato sauce, hot oil, and sea salt mingle in the air. Boats buzz upon the water. Daily life goes on.

"I'm happy you're happy, but I'm *most* happy that our luggage is here," I say.

CHAPTER 3

I flop down on the bed, stretch my arms above my head, and close my eyes until I startle awake at sensing a presence standing next to me. "What?"

Karen looks down at me. "Please don't get too comfy. If we fall asleep now, it'll throw off our sleep schedule tonight. Let's go for a walk."

I roll onto my side, take a deep breath, and slowly push myself off of the bed that beckons me to stay. I put on my shoes, and we make our way out of the room. Once downstairs, Karen and I emerge onto the street to a mixture of joy and chaos. Music, laughter, and brightly colored costumed revelers in constant movement. I suggest we walk in a straight line for now.

Karen happily window-shops for ideas on presents to take home. She's not disappointed at the number of shops available. She wraps her arm in mine as we amble along, the street gently curving to reveal the Grand Canal before us. We make our way to St. Mark's Square, or as it's locally known, Piazza San Marco. It's iconic in Venice.

"Let's stop and have coffee at Caffè Florian," Karen says. "I read in the guidebook that it's been a mainstay in Venice since 1720."

We find a table and each order an espresso. I sink back into the chair. Karen sways gently to the music from the live band in front of the café and rubs her fingertips across the top of my hand as the waiter places our order on the table.

A panorama of costumes, colors, and textures parade through the area. My eyes rove over the crowd when in a single fluid movement, I'm out of my seat and standing straight up.

Concern sweeps over Karen's face. "Dan, are you okay?"

Her voice snaps my attention back. "What? No, I just saw Dr. Virk."

She stands up and swivels her head from side to side. "The doctor from our trip to France? Are you sure? Where?"

"Positive! Surprisingly, or maybe not so as he's a doctor, but he's wearing a plague doctor costume."

Karen's brow furrows. "Then how can you be sure it's him?"

"He pulled his mask off while he was resting against the wall. We made eye contact and recognized each other immediately. He put his mask back on and disappeared into the crowd. He's in Venice, *with us*."

My mind races. This is not a good thing. What's he doing here? He had escaped France by helicopter after the murders before he could be arrested. Is this where he planned to reinvent himself?

"I'm sure he'll want to avoid us, so there shouldn't be any danger," Karen says, taking my hand, her eyes pleading with me to not obsess over this development.

"He needs to answer for his part of what happened in France," I snap back.

She withdraws her hand and averts her eyes. I want to give

her the vacation she dreams of, but Dr. Virk being free bothers my sense of justice. I could run into the crowd, pulling off plague doctor masks from everyone I see. That plan is readily discarded.

Karen looks at me, her lips pressed tightly together. "If Dr. Virk's being here is going to bother you, I don't want to spend the entire trip fearing he's in the crowd. I propose a compromise."

"I'm listening."

"Talk to Lorenzo. He's a crime reporter. Maybe he knows a local detective you can talk to about what happened in France and let the Italian authorities deal with it."

"That's a good idea," I reply. I shoot her a sideways glance and a sly smile. "But you know I'm going to look at every plague doctor with suspicion, right?"

"Yeah, I know that," she agrees. "However, I'd like to avoid you trying to take the masks off everyone you see."

Wow, it's like she read my mind. She knows me too well.

I call Lorenzo's cell and explain where we are, that I have a situation I need to discuss with him. He agrees to meet us at Caffè Florian. We sip our drinks, but I can't help scanning the crowd.

Lorenzo arrives and drops into a chair. He leans back. "You are happy here in Venice, yes?"

"Yes," I reply hesitantly. "But there is something I may need your help with." I explain the situation with seeing Dr. Virk here and some of the tragic deaths that happened in France. Lorenzo sits upright with his elbows on the tabletop. I finish my story. Lorenzo snaps his fingers for a waiter and orders a coffee.

"I will make a call." Lorenzo pulls his cell phone from his pocket, dials, and speaks Italian. I catch the words *omicidio* and *commissario*, which translate to me as homicide and commissioner. He dramatically cuts off the call. "My friend will be right over." He raises his cup. *"Cin, cin."*

I'm amazed that Lorenzo has that much influence with the police.

Karen and I simultaneously verbalize, "Cheers."

"Now, Dan and Karen, I have found you a guide to give you a private tour while in Venice. His name is Paul Aiello." He explains some of the places we will be touring.

I lean toward him to ask questions as a shadow falls across the table. I turn my head and see a familiar face. It's Caputo.

He nods in acknowledgement. *"Bueno sera."*

"Sit, sit," Lorenzo says impatiently. "Dan, you explain."

The *commissario* glides into a chair with the grace of a cat, effortlessly. I repeat what I told Lorenzo regarding the situation in France and the role Dr. Virk played. I like Caputo. His eyes are intense but not challenging. I believe he heard everything that was said, is processing it for validity, and is not revealing anything before he knows all the facts in the case and has a plan. That's what I would do.

He draws in a long breath through his nose, then releases a sigh. "You are sure it was this Dr. Virk?"

"Yeah, we made eye contact, and we both knew," I reply.

"I will contact the French police to see if they are interested in him, but I have no authority to arrest him in Italy if he has not committed a crime here or entered the country illegally."

I'm annoyed at the thought that not much will happen but

want to engage the local police on a positive note, just in case. "Thank you for coming and listening to my story. Can I buy you a drink?"

Caputo nods with a slight smile, stating, "I am done working today."

Before I can catch the waiter's attention, Lorenzo snaps his fingers repeatedly in the air. I'm annoyed but repress asking him to not do that. A waiter scurries to the table and takes the order from Caputo, who reclines in his chair.

I lean forward. "I can't help but ask. Was Anna's death natural causes?"

He narrows his eyes, but never breaks eye contact. I'm sure he's considering whether or not to answer, or what to answer.

There's a slight shrug of his shoulders. "We have nothing for certain."

"And?" I give an encouraging nod.

A sly grin creases his lips. "I am suspicious but will wait for the lab report to know. Murder is rare in Venice. Criminals here are more, how you say, opportunistic. Pickpockets, car burglary, stealing items from distracted tourists."

"So, was it the pins on the floor?"

"We are testing many things," Caputo answers flatly.

Lorenzo taps the table. "Pins? What pins?"

"Large pearl-headed straight pins," Caputo replies. "Very expensive. Anna had been using them shortly before her death. She had blood on two of her fingers, so she must have cut herself. As I said, we are testing the pins." He leans forward, and his dark eyes laser-focus on me. "Will I find your fingerprints on the box?"

I shake my head. "No. I checked for a pulse, realized she was dead, and stepped out of the area."

A twitch of his mouth is his only response. I can't read his face or body language to tell if he's satisfied with my answer.

"So, it could be murder by poison?" I ask.

Caputo's eyes turn darker. "I did not say that."

Lorenzo breaks in. "I did not touch anything. I was not even in that room." He waves his hands in front of us.

Caputo snaps his head toward Lorenzo. "Pfft."

I repress a smile at that response.

Karen touches my arm, reminding me that this is *not* my investigation. I decide to switch gears. "How long have you been with the police?"

Caputo waves his hand dismissively. "Many years. I started in a small mountain village with simple crimes but took the position I have now five or six years ago." He asks me about my career, and I explain how I started as a patrol officer, but fell in love with being a detective and doing my own evidence work. Time melts away as we compare stories and laugh about how much of policing is the same, no matter where.

Dusk has settled. The exterior lights of the businesses in the area add a warm, yellow glow. Caputo excuses himself to head home.

Karen taps my hand. "I think the jet lag is catching up with me. Can we head back to the bed-and-breakfast?"

"I will walk with you as it is on my way home," Lorenzo states more than offers. "I will pick you up tomorrow for your final fitting."

"It's not necessary for Arielle to do that. She's grieving.

I'm sure the dress will be fine if we just pick it up," Karen says.

"*Signora*, no. Arielle will do this. I have asked her." Lorenzo waves at us to follow him. "Come now."

Karen throws up her hands, and we follow him to the bed-and-breakfast and wave goodbye. I trudge behind Karen to our room. Both of us change and crawl into bed. Karen cuddles into me, the smell of perfume lingering on her skin. I close my eyes, willing myself to fall asleep, but I can't. Motives, means, opportunities ping-pong around my brain.

"What's wrong?" Karen's voice pierces the darkness.

"Uh, nothing."

She pushes herself into a sitting position. "I can feel you thinking. So, something's bothering you."

I throw the blankets to the side and sit up next to her. "If Anna was murdered, then by who? Why use a box of poisoned pins? It seems so elaborate."

"We don't know what caused Anna's death. Let's say hypothetically the pins are the murder weapon. Maybe they were meant for Arielle, or for both of them. We can check on who has issues with Anna and/or Arielle tomorrow, but for now can we try to get some sleep?"

We both lie back down. I focus on slowing my breathing and being relaxed, and after what seems like a long time, I feel myself drift off to sleep.

CHAPTER 4

Early-morning light seeps through the curtains. Karen and I shower and dress before heading downstairs promptly at 8:00 a.m. The smell of coffee and eggs brings me joy and leads me to the dining room. I'm starving.

The room is bright and welcoming. A soft blue wallpaper with white apple blossoms covers the walls, and place settings don the surfaces of four two-person square tables. The room is empty except for Katherine sitting on a wooden chair against the far wall, engrossed in her phone. I'm surprised to see her after yesterday. Based on her positioning in the room, I think she works here. I do notice she's wearing an impressive diamond tennis bracelet. I wonder where that came from as working here can't pay that well. Boyfriend, maybe? Karen and I find a table and sit down.

Arthur Ravenscraft walks into the room, coughing, pipe in hand. He tries to light it without success. "Katherine, get off that blasted thing. Can't you see we have paying guests?"

Katherine releases a dramatic sigh and lays her phone down in no apparent rush. She meanders to a serving cart, picks up two white carafes, and comes to our table. "Would you like coffee or tea?" We both order coffee.

"Hello, again," Karen says. "I hope we're okay after what happened with Anna."

Katherine shrugs. "Fine."

I join the conversation. "You work here?"

A barely perceivable nod. "Lady Ravenscraft is my mother."

"Well, it's nice she has you to help," Karen says.

"I guess. I'm cheap help." She turns and places the carafes on the cart before heading back to her chair.

Karen looks at me and mouths, "Whatever."

When you're happy in your work, it shows, I think sarcastically.

A full plate in hand, Arthur strides to our table and extends his arm. "Lord Arthur Ravenscraft. Good of you to be here."

I stand slightly and return the handshake. Guess he doesn't remember meeting us yesterday.

Harriet Ravenscraft sweeps into the room with effortless ease. She throws an icy glare at her daughter before making her way to our table. "How was your first night's sleep?"

"Wonderful," we reply in unison.

"Good to hear it. Arthur, let them enjoy their breakfast," she snaps. "This day will go much more smoothly if you just do as you're told. Take your plate to the kitchen."

Arthur coughs and ambles out of the room.

"I placed the itinerary on your dresser last night. Not sure if you've seen it?"

She was in our room last night. Why? That makes me uncomfortable. Contemplating whether to say something, I glance at her, but she appears unfazed. I decide to let it go . . . for now.

"I skimmed it briefly this morning. It looks like amazing fun," Karen replies.

"Please look it over and make note of the activities. Tonight is a more intimate gathering of select people. No more than ten or twelve. The other ball is more formal. I expect closer to thirty. Please be aware that both are full-costumed events. I ask that you arrive promptly for each event. Good to see you both again." A precision turn, and she heads toward the kitchen.

I roll my eyes at Karen, who pats my hand in understanding. We tuck into the food, which is delicious. Breakfast takes a while, partly because Katherine is less than attentive with refilling our coffee. I clean my plate and finish Karen's leftovers. No wasted food here.

Karen leans back in her chair, sipping from her cup. "We should hurry before Lorenzo comes to take us to see Arielle."

We're just about to enter our room when a maid steps out of the room next door. Is that Joanna? When I take a step closer to her to introduce myself, she moves back into the room and closes the door. That's odd, but I dismiss it for now.

Karen grabs her wallet off our bed. I double-check that I have my phone and wallet. At the door, Karen stops. "I really hate imposing on Arielle for this last fitting, especially now."

"I agree, but Lorenzo is pushing her to do it. So let's get it done and leave her alone to grieve."

Lorenzo is in the lobby whispering with Arthur, who pats Lorenzo's arm. Katherine walks past them both toward the front door.

"Where do you think you're off to?" Arthur bellows

at Katherine. "Have you finished helping your mother with breakfast?"

She spins and spits out, "That's who I *am* helping. Mother has ordered more flowers for tonight, and I'm picking them up."

Harriet steps into the hall. "Arthur, let her get going. Paul is coming. I don't have time for delays."

Arthur's brows furrow. "Who?"

A deep sigh escapes from Harriet. "Paul Aiello, the travel blogger. He's doing a piece on Casa de Inglese that he hopes to sell to a travel magazine. It could mean the kind of exposure this place needs."

"Fine, fine. If that's what you want. Katherine, stop standing there and get going." Arthur turns and heads for the library, muttering, "Such rut. Blogging, posting, social mediaing. Nonsense, if you ask me."

"I didn't ask you," Harriet says after him. "Paul only goes to the most exclusive places. He's coming here, and that's that."

Karen and I exchange uncomfortable glances.

Lorenzo beams at us. "*Buongiorno*. You are ready, *signora*, *signore*?" He heads out the door. We quickly follow him, weaving through the streets and alleyways to Arielle's shop.

"Arielle, Arielle!" he calls out as he enters the shop. She steps out from the back. "The *signora* needs her fitting."

"*Buongiorno*," Arielle says softly. "Come. Your dress is ready."

Karen whispers, "I'm so sorry to impose at this time." Arielle silently nods.

Lorenzo waves his hand in the direction of the curtain. Arielle steps behind it and returns holding a tan garment bag. She unzips it to reveal a beautiful, deep-green velvet dress with gold trim.

"*Signora*, come," Arielle says. "You must try on, please."

Karen follows her to the back of the shop. I wander around, looking at masks, hats, and costumes. Each in amazing colors and details. Moments later, Karen emerges in full costume. The dress hugs her curves. After forty years together, she can still take my breath away. The dress is complemented by a gold mask, its sequin scrolls and feathers at the top in the same green. Her shoulder-length brown hair falls in soft curls. The mask is a perfect accent. I love how she looks.

"You're beautiful," I say. "You'll turn heads when you enter the room. I'll have to be careful, or some Italian nobleman will steal you away." I take her hands and spin her around.

"*Bellissima, signora*," Lorenzo states.

Karen squeezes Arielle's hand. "I feel like a princess. Thank you."

"*Sì, sì*," Arielle mutters. "Come, let us get you undressed."

Moments later, Karen and Arielle emerge from behind the curtain. Arielle hands me a flat, black mask embossed with Romanesque figures and symbols. Detailed but understated. She places everything in a hanging bag.

"Again, we're sorry for your loss," Karen adds as Lorenzo ushers us out the door and back to our bed-and-breakfast. He says his goodbyes as we enter the inn. Karen hangs the garment bag in the closet of our room.

We review the itinerary Harriet left for us.

"I'm glad we have our costumes. It's exciting," Karen says.

My phone rings, and it's *Commissario* Caputo. The

information he gives me is not what I want to hear. Frustration wells up in me as I hang up.

Karen shoots me a puzzled look.

"That was Caputo. He contacted the French authorities, who confirmed they're interested in Dr. Saeed Virk, but no one by that name has entered Italy since we left France. He questioned the certainty of my sighting Dr. Virk, but I assured him there was no mistake. I guess at this time there is nothing he can do." My mind searches for other ways to possibly locate Virk while he's in Italy.

Karen sits next to me. "Dan, you saw the guy for a few seconds. Are you really sure it was him?"

"Yes!" I snap. "He hasn't even bothered to change his appearance and flew away with three million euros. That can buy a new identity, so what name is he using now?" I mentally scroll through other people and resources in law enforcement. A few names come to mind. If Caputo won't help, I'll call them and ask if there's anything that can be done to locate Virk with his new name.

"Well, I doubt he's using Dr. I. M. Hurt." Karen smirks, recalling his alias from France. "We'll be vigilant, but not paranoid. Right?" Her eyes implore me to agree.

I nod.

"We have a few hours before the party tonight. Let's explore Venice some more and try to find our way to Il Sogno for lunch," Karen offers.

I pull myself off the bed and put my shoes on. Once we're outside, Karen takes my hand. The salt air hits my nose while music and laughter envelop me. I silently repeat to myself, "Relax. You're on vacation and not a cop here."

After an hour or so of walking—or more like serious people dodging—we find ourselves at the restaurant. Andrea greets us with a smile, grabs a couple of menus, and shows us to a waterside table. Karen and I are discussing what we might like to order when shouting interrupts us. Through the open restaurant door, a red-faced, blond-haired woman is yelling at Andrea and stabbing her finger into the center of his chest. She wears a chef's toque and white jacket. He stands still, head hung down, avoiding any eye contact with her until she throws up her hands and stomps into the kitchen. Wow, she works here and talks to the owner that way? That is one angry woman.

Andrea scurries to our table, blushing, but with a smile pressed to his lips. We place our order, then Karen and I watch life on the canal.

"It never ceases to amaze me, the spectacle of the boats, the people, and the architecture," she says.

I'm lost in thought. Do the residents see this beauty? Andrea's sudden appearance at my elbow jolts my attention. He places our plates on the table. I wasn't aware of my surroundings. Could Dr. Virk appear without my notice? Karen looks at me questioningly.

I smile. "Daydreaming." Skepticism flashes in her eyes, but she doesn't push for more.

The woman is yelling from the door of the restaurant, again. Words like "*idiota*" and "*deficiente*" can be heard. Andrea hurries toward her just as she flings a menu at him. She misses. He motions for her to move toward the kitchen. Patrons strain to see the drama unfolding. Some shake their heads; others focus on their plates of food.

We tuck into our lunch. Andrea returns with our bill.

Karen touches his arm. "Everything okay?"

He draws a deep breath. "*Sì, sì.* Mia Teresa. She is *appassionata.* It is what makes her a great chef."

"Oh, she's your chef," I reply.

"*Sì* and *mia sposa.* She is very tired today and gets upset."

It must be difficult to work together, especially if she feels entitled to treat him with such disrespect. I feel for him. I'm glad I'm here with Karen.

CHAPTER 5

Karen and I open the door of our bed-and-breakfast to a rush of noise. Dozens of people scurry through the main floor with various party accessories. Chairs, plates, glassware, and flowers move at something approaching the speed of light. We make our way to the stairs, pause, and listen. Lady Ravenscraft is shouting orders and pointing to various staff.

White cloth drapes, drawn up with gold and white pom-poms at precise intervals, form symmetrical swags on the staircase and balcony. A long banquet table is centered in the front hall while round tables with white tablecloths fill in be-tween. Each is graced with a tall golden candelabra holding five white pillar candles and a ring of white roses at the base. A waiter measures the placement of each utensil.

The crash of the front door grabs everyone's attention. In steps a man with stark white hair in the style of a shih tzu, ponytail on top and long, shaggy sides. He sports a black, double-breasted jacket with silver buttons, matching bell-bot-toms, purple-tinted glasses, and an elaborate camera around his neck.

Harriet glides across the hall. "Paul, so good of you to come. This is a real treat."

He silently waves her off, walks around the room, points the camera, and takes several pictures.

"Please let me know if there's anything you need set up differently." I'm not sure, but I may've heard Harriet cooing at him. She shoots a glare in our direction. I wonder if we're not beautiful enough to stay. I repress a smirk and take Karen's hand. We head to our room to relax before the ball tonight and not be a hindrance to the workers.

Karen turns to me. "It looks amazing downstairs. I'm excited for the party tonight."

"I'm excited too," I say, but I'm more concerned with the number of costumed people who will be moving around me. What if Dr. Virk, or whatever his name is now, is invited? Is Karen in danger, or the other guests, or *me*? I lie on the bed, mentally reviewing possible weapons available, if needed, to defend the guests. Cutlery, candleholders, bottles. However, Dr. Virk had killed in less obvious ways. Poison seems a more viable option for him. At parties, people relax and tend to forgive being bumped into, so I plan to be vigilant for people around Karen and myself.

"Karen, keep an eye on anything you eat or drink tonight, please." I say.

She kisses my forehead. "Thank you for the concern, but Smart Girl 101 is 'always be aware.' To ease your mind, though, I promise I won't let another man buy me a drink tonight."

I drop my head to the pillow, breathe deeply, and envision enjoying the evening. A snore awakens me, and I look around the room. Karen has her costume on.

"How long have I been asleep?" I ask.

"A couple of hours," she replies. "Could you help, please?"

I zip up the back of her full-length green velvet dress. Her brown hair falls to her shoulders in soft curls. She finishes off the look with the gold sequined mask trimmed with green feathers.

A quick shower revives me. I pull on black pants, black shoes, a white shirt, a gold-and-green geometrically patterned vest, a long black cape, and a black embossed mask. In the mirror, I'm pleased with my look. Not bad for guys my age. Well, at least I have all my hair.

We step into the corridor and head downstairs. The front hall and dining room have been transformed. Candles fill the rooms with a warm glow and the scent of lilies of the valley. Soft, operatic music wafts through the air. Lady Ravenscraft has changed into a perfectly fitted, full-length ball gown of black satin, with a black-and-gold floral brocade jacket that bells out at the bottom. Black shoes, a mask, and a round, feathered hat complete her look.

Her outfit is a contrast to the room's color scheme. Does she need to stand out? We make eye contact.

"There you are. So glad you're punctual," Harriet states. "The other guests will be arriving shortly. Find something to drink and please *do* mingle this evening." She turns and heads to the kitchen. Arthur Ravenscraft meanders in from the library. He's sporting a military costume of black pantaloons, white socks, black shoes, and a white shirt ruffled at the collar and cuffs. His black-and-gold vest with its knee-length jacket are the same material and design as his wife's. He's topped the outfit with a classic three-pointed admiral's hat in black with gold trim.

He searches for a pocket to deposit his pipe in as he extends his hand. "Lord Arthur Ravenscraft. So glad you're here."

I smile and shake his hand as I introduce Karen and me . . . for the third time.

"Be sure to get plenty to eat and drink this evening. You've paid for it." He lets out a roar of laughter.

The front door opens, and costumed guests file in. Karen and I move so my back is against the wall and I have a clear view of the room. Old cop habits. Arthur is off to welcome his guests with the same greeting. Out of the corner of my eye, I notice movement on the stairs. Coming down them is a couple. My eyes remain on them. The man is dressed in a plague doctor costume. My mind races with possible scenarios that include tackling the person and ripping the mask off. A warm hand slides up my back. Karen reads my mind. I inhale deeply through my nose and release a sigh, forcing myself to try and relax.

"I'd like to introduce myself to our fellow lodgers to see if they speak English," Karen says, gliding past me, which raises my anxiety. I'm still assessing what I want to do while keeping an eye on Karen, who waves me over.

"Dan, this is John. He's a British ex-pat and a friend of Arthur's."

John extends his hand. Tentatively, I shake it and introduce myself.

John removes his mask. "Damn hard to hear in this bloody thing. What did you say, old man?" Face-to-face with a middle-aged, balding man, I calm down. No Dr. Virk here. I repeat my name.

John introduces us to his wife, Linda. She's dressed in a purple, sequined gown with matching mask and hat. We make our way to the bar area and get glasses of champagne all around. As more guests arrive, I repeatedly check the room. Thankfully I don't see anyone else dressed in the plague doctor costume, but would Dr. Virk be dressed the same, or would he have a different outfit?

As we stand by the bar, John, Linda, Karen, and I are discussing general topics of where we are from, occupations, and what brought us to Venice when I sense a presence lurking behind me. I turn sharply and find a tall figure dressed in black clothes and a floor-length black cape. Dark eyes stare at me from his striking white mask. "*Bueno sera, Signore* Novice."

My breath catches in my throat as my mind searches for the owner of the voice. He raises his mask and winks. I chuckle. It's *Commissario* Caputo.

"I am sorry if I made you nervous. It is easy to hide during Carnival."

"Let's get you a drink," I offer. I whisper to Karen that it's Caputo. He dips his head to her, then introduces himself to John and Linda, minus his police title. Our group moves to a table as servers bring out platters of food and set them on the long banquet tables. The smells of warm bread and tomato sauce reach my nose. Andrea scurries behind the servers, rearranging plates, then wiping the edges of each with a white towel. He snaps a nod as he views the table. Andrea and Teresa are catering the event.

Arthur joins our group. I look up to scan the balcony. Paul Aiello is photographing the event from it. He points the camera, leans back dramatically, snaps a picture, then appears to review the image. He meanders along the corridor our room is on. Minutes pass before he reappears. Were pictures the only thing he was taking?

A woman stops briefly at our table. She is wearing a silver hoop dress with a high ruffled collar, her silver sequined mask showcasing a silver snake on one side and a crescent moon on the other. "*Bueno sera.*" She softly rubs Caputo's shoulder before heading into the dining room. A grin curls the corners of his mouth. "Danielle Ricci, the local pharmacist." I raise my eyebrows. Caputo shrugs. I remember meeting her at the pharmacy when Lorenzo picked up his medication.

Waitstaff fill our glasses with more champagne.

The front door opens widely as another guest steps inside. He throws his arms out widely. "*Bueno sera. Mi scusi,*" booms Lorenzo's voice. If that wasn't enough of an entrance, his costume is. He's dressed in glittering gold lamé from the full-length jacket, pants, vest, oversized bow tie, and embossed mask. He even dons a white wig with gold glitter in it.

I catch the glare of Harriet's eyes. She recovers instantly and presses a tight smile on her face. "Lorenzo, I thought you weren't coming."

"*Sì, sì.* I thought not, but now I am."

"Well, let's carry on then," she remarks.

Lorenzo strolls around the room, shaking hands, slapping others on the back, boisterously laughing. He makes his way to Caputo and speaks in Italian to him. Caputo points to the dining room. Lorenzo pats his shoulder and walks away.

A frown creases my face.

"He is looking for Danielle." Caputo says.

Harriet announces that guests are welcome to start eating. Arthur abruptly gets up, heads for the buffet table, and approaches a woman in a navy-blue dress and mask. He grabs her arm, but she yanks herself free from his grasp. They stand facing each other, their noses barely separated. I can't hear what's being said, but Arthur's neck is a vivid red. The woman slams down the plate she was holding and yells, "I hate you!" She runs up the stairs. Arthur stomps back to our table, muttering, "Damn impertinent."

"Who?" John asks.

"Katherine, my stepdaughter. Lazy girl. No help. No help at all. Puts herself first in line for food. Impertinent, I say."

John calmly says, "Not in our day. We were expected to work. Nothing handed to us. Remember our first day in the army?"

Arthur laughs out loud. His shoulders relax, and he opens his clenched fists. He and John reminisce of their time together in the British army. I smile, since much of what they're saying is like my time in the U.S. army.

Caputo leans into me. "I have thought of what you said about this Dr. Virk, what happened in France, and what he is doing here. I am checking passport entrances with the same initials." He snorts a laugh. "Maybe he would not want to change his monogramed shirts."

I cock my head to face him and nod approval. He's going to help. Caputo leans back in his chair, fingertips pressed together, and his eyes sweep the room. Cop habits are the same in any culture.

Lorenzo returns. "I cannot find Dani. She is not here or in the dining room or anywhere. I must speak to her. Has anyone seen her?"

Everyone replies, "No."

Lorenzo wanders toward the library.

Linda excuses herself from the table, explaining that she forgot her medication in her room. Everyone else moves to the buffet table. While I wait in line, I survey the pastas, marinara alfredo, and pesto sauces, the platters of antipasti, and rolls. I reach for a serving spoon when a primal scream penetrates the air.

"We've been robbed!" Linda shrieks from the balcony.

CHAPTER 6

Caputo drops his plate and heads for the stairs. Instinctively, I follow. Linda points to an open door. Caputo eases it the rest of the way open with his elbow. I'm two steps behind him.

John embraces Linda, saying, "What happened?"

"I went to take my medication and the room was a mess. Drawers ajar. The pouch for my jewelry was open on the bed. I'm positive I took out the jewelry I'm wearing now and put it back in our suitcase. Everything is gone. My mother's pearls and the sapphire ring. The diamond earrings my grandmother gave me for our wedding." Tears roll down Linda's face. John hugs her tight.

Harriet Ravenscraft pushes past me into the room. "This is intolerable. Who would do this?"

Caputo blocks her way with his body and moves towards her, causing her to step back into the hallway. "This is a crime scene. Everyone stay where you are," he loudly announces, then turns to me and quietly adds, "I will call for a forensics team." Grabbing his phone, he pushes a button, and rapid Italian soon begins. Guests are gathering at the bottom of the stairs.

Arthur Ravenscraft pushes his way up the steps. "Let me through. What is the meaning of this?" He bends over, gasping for air as he reaches me. I put an arm out for him to lean on, hoping he doesn't pass out. Red-faced, he looks at me, spitting out, "This is impertinent, I say. Who is to blame for this?"

"Arthur!" Harriet glares at him. "There's nothing for you to do here. Go back downstairs. I'll talk to the police."

He lowers his head, mumbling, "Very well. Carry on, my dear." He ambles his way back down.

I look over the railing and make eye contact with Karen. She gives me a weak smile as she comes toward me, motioning me closer. I meet her a few steps from the top.

"I don't mean to sound self-centered," Karen says quietly, "but would you be able to check our room and the others? John and Linda may not be the only victims."

"Will do."

Caputo joins us. He asks Karen to accompany us as we search our room.

Inside the room, Karen checks the small, black velvet jeweler's box she uses. "Nothing's missing, but I never bring anything expensive on vacation."

Caputo nods. "Please wait downstairs," he says.

Harriet confirms that the remaining room was a last-minute cancellation, so Katherine is staying in it.

Were John and Linda targeted? Who would know that she kept expensive items unsecured?

People remove their masks and strain for a view of what's happening. Happily for me, there is no Dr. Virk. However, noticeably absent are Lorenzo, Katherine, and Dani, the pharmacist. *Why aren't they curious about the situation?*

Caputo's back inside John and Linda's room while I

anxiously wait for his backup. *What's taking so long?* After what seems an inordinate amount of time, uniformed officers and equipment arrive and are dispatched to various tasks by Caputo. The first is to secure the exits. I fear that some of the guests were able to escape before giving a statement.

Another quick look around from the top of the stairs, and I spot Lorenzo at one of the tables, eating a plate of food. Katherine is sitting next to him. When did they get there? I'm positive that table was empty when I looked a few minutes ago. Dani is still missing. My knees resent my hurried pace down the stairs to search for her. Karen squeezes my arm as I pass her, but I don't stop as I make my way through the crowd and toward the library. Movement out of the corner of my eye stops me as I catch Dani wandering out of the kitchen. She's removed her elaborate mask. Has she been there the whole time? Why didn't she come out to see what was happening? I'm about to ask her that when Lorenzo yells her name. She hurries past me and sits between him and Katherine, speaking in hushed tones.

Karen comes up behind me. "Dan, this isn't your investigation. I'm sure we'll need to give statements tonight."

I drop my head, acknowledging that she's right. Caputo and a young officer—they're getting younger by the year—move to the library door. Caputo looks inside and snaps orders to the officer, who clicks his heels and spins around, his back to the library, facing the hall. I'd love to be a fly on the wall for the interviews.

Karen rubs her hand on my back and says, "Well, at least it isn't a murder. Please don't get involved in this." I hear the plea in her voice and pat her arm, but it doesn't stop me from observing everyone's behaviors and writing notes on napkins as I'm sitting at a table. I plan to innocently share them with Caputo when I give my statement. Karen sighs. She's aware of what I'm doing.

Lorenzo, Katherine, and Danielle are still at their table with their heads close together. Katherine points to the top of the staircase with her right arm. Lorenzo pushes it back down, shaking his head. Dani presses a tight smile on her lips. She makes eye contact with me, anger clearly visible, and doesn't break it until Lorenzo says something to her.

John sits beside Linda at a table close to the library door, his arm around her shoulders, talking to her softly. Linda sobs into a shredded paper napkin.

"My heart breaks for Linda," Karen says. "The loss of something with sentimental value is worse than the monetary loss. I hope the things are found."

Rarely are burglary items recovered unless the thief makes a mistake, such as trying to pawn it to an honest shop owner. I'll have to ask Caputo what the laws for pawnbrokers are here.

Linda is the first to be interviewed. She shuffles into the library, still clutching her napkin. John glances up and scans the dining room. I give him a look, trying to convey my sorrow at his present situation. He shrugs his shoulders.

The crowd is moving around the room. Some take seats, others pace, others decide to eat. The tone of the room moves from curiosity to more and more vocal frustration, all under the wary eyes of officers posted at each entrance, preventing anyone from escaping.

Dani and Katherine move toward the stairs. An officer puts his hand up and shakes his head.

"I want to use the bathroom in my room," Katherine snaps. I don't catch the officer's reply. Dani speaks to him in Italian, but his facial expression never changes. Apparently even his native language doesn't sway him. He motions for both of them to return to their seats.

Karen and I help ourselves to the dinner offerings, and Karen grabs a bottle of champagne for us to share. We position ourselves at a table with our backs to the wall. Surprisingly, the food is still warm. Two bites into the shrimp scampi and I realize I'm really hungry.

"This chicken alfredo is amazing," Karen gushes. "I feel bad that this feast prepared by Teresa and Andrea isn't being enjoyed." We both finish everything on our plates. I'm considering if it would be in poor taste to go back for seconds, given that this is a crime scene.

Lorenzo suddenly jumps to his feet, pushes his way to the library, and furiously pounds on the door. He steps back at the suddenness of its opening and speaks in short, clipped sentences with his index finger up in Caputo's face. Caputo's response is a guttural growl and a swift slam of the door.

Lorenzo huffs loudly and flops into the nearest chair, his arms crossed against his chest. I suppress a laugh. Apparently, he's very used to getting his way.

Time creeps along as individuals are summoned into the library for formal interviews. Verbalizations in several languages increase in volume from the guests. The officers stationed at various points in the room appear unimpressed by them. Once the guests are interviewed, they're free to leave.

Finally, Karen and I take our turns. During mine, I relay

what I know and what I've observed, which has not been much. I hand my napkin notes to Caputo, who laughs and shakes his head.

"Once a police officer, always one?" he questions.

"Yes, and in any language," I reply.

I share my observations that Lorenzo, Katherine, and Dani had been missing when the robbery was discovered, but that there could have been other guests that I didn't recognize as well.

Caputo snickers and relaxes his shoulders. "I am sad to say that recently Venice has had several jewel robberies. However, I cannot see Lorenzo as a, how you say, 'cat thief.'"

"Burglar. It's 'cat burglar.'"

"Yes, that. Dani, she is a pharmacist. Her mother and father built a good business and gave it to her to run. I do not see her doing this. Katherine, I do not know. She came here when her mother and stepfather bought this place."

Karen and I are some of the last to be interviewed and are officially released to our room. The hall is nearly empty now except for Harriet as she carries platters of food to the kitchen. Karen and I try to help, but she steps in front of us. "Please stop. I know how I want things done here." It's been an anticlimactic end to our first official Carnival ball.

We trudge up the steps, change out of our costumes, and tumble into bed. I have dreams where I'm pursuing masked bandits up flights of stairs, through dark streets, but am never able to identify them, until I startle awake. Morning light filters through the windows. I work to slow my breathing. Karen is still asleep beside me, so I slide out of bed and into the bathroom for a shower.

As I reenter the bedroom, Karen sits up in bed, still half-asleep. "I had the weirdest dream," she says. "I was following a trail of gold glitter to a hallway. A bright, silver moon was shining at the end of the hall, but dark shadows were darting in and out of the bedrooms. Each door was different, and they opened and closed on their own. I tried to find a way out, but the rooms didn't make sense."

I hug her tight. "I was thinking whether or not we should stay here after what happened last night."

She pushes herself up to a sitting position. "Dan, a robbery can happen anywhere. If thieves target a place or person, then it happens. We've talked about never bringing anything that draws attention to yourself, or anything you can't afford to lose."

"Yeah, but there's been a murder, and Dr. Virk, *and* now this. I don't like it."

Karen sighs. "Well, I don't have anything worth stealing. So, we plan to be aware and safe, but not paranoid. Deal?"

I'm reluctant to agree. "I still don't like it, but deal. Let's head down to breakfast. My treat."

She places a hand over her heart. "You're too kind. I want to see how Harriet's doing." Showered and dressed, we leave our room.

Karen stops at the top of the stairs. While looking below, she sighs sadly.

"Is something wrong?" I say, trying to read her facial expression.

She hesitates before speaking. "No. Just a little sad to see the remains of what a great night should've been."

I peer down at the chafing dishes, cleaned and set upon the white linen tablecloths draped perfectly across each buffet table. Harriet must have worked for hours to restore this level of order. My thoughts are interrupted by Andrea scurrying around the tables, adjusting the placement of each item on them.

He jumps at the sight of us. "Boungiorno."

"Boungiorno," Karen and I call back in unison as we start down the stairs. Teresa joins him and glares at the table setting before yanking various platters off the table and shoving them into Andrea's hands. Through clenched teeth, she hisses an Italian command that I can't make out. Andrea hangs his head. I pity his life with this woman. Not wanting to get in the way, Karen and I quickly move into the dining room. We're the first to arrive this morning. No Katherine.

Harriet sweeps in with two carafes and makes her way to us. "Coffee or tea?"

We both order coffee, so she places a carafe on our table. John and Linda make their way to a table on the other side of the room, never making eye contact with us.

"How are you doing this morning?" Karen asks Harriet quietly.

Harriet stares at Karen with bewilderment. "Doing?"

"The robbery last night and the police being here."

Harriet waves her hand. "Oh, that. Well, needs must. Carry on." She moves to John and Linda's table.

Karen looks at me with disbelief in her eyes. I'm bothered by Harriet's lack of concern that her guests were victims of a crime in her house. I look over to John, who nods acknowledgement. I return the gesture. We're waiting for our breakfast to arrive when snippets of an angry conversation drift in from the hall.

"He doesn't see anything in you. He's a man of class and distinction." The voice belongs to Arthur Ravenscraft.

"Leave me alone, old man!" Katherine shouts back.

"Lazy cow," snaps Arthur before bursting into the dining room. Everyone's heads snap up. Arthur stomps to John's side. "Sorry, old friend. My stepdaughter and I never got on. Caught her in the hall mooning over him. As if she'd have a chance of marrying him." He drops into a chair at the table.

John opens his mouth as if to say something, then closes it. Harriet places plates of food in front of both John and Linda. Arthur is muttering more to himself than anyone, oblivious to the icy glare from his wife. John bows his head and tucks into his breakfast while Linda pushes food around the plate.

Harriet speaks to Arthur. "You need to let people eat in peace."

"Sorry, ole boy. Must get on," he replies, his cheeks flushed pink with embarrassment, then moves toward the hall.

Karen and I make brief eye contact. I feel as bad for him as I do Andrea. Karen jumps as Katherine appears at our table and drops off our plates, and I do mean drops. She stands there looking at something across the room toward the doorway. My eyes follow her line of sight. Barely visible is Mario Giudice, who's speaking with Teresa. Teresa's facial features have softened as she looks at Mario. A smile has replaced her clenched teeth.

My mind assesses the implications. So that's who Arthur

was referring to, Katherine and Mario, or at least Katherine wanting to be with Mario. His mother Anna's death may aid him in pressuring Arielle to sell the costume shop. Katherine did bring in the box of poisoned pins that she said she happened to find outside the shop. Are they co-conspirators, or is Katherine clearing a path for her to pursue Mario? I regard them both as suspects for now.

"Dan!" Karen's voice breaks my thoughts.

"What?"

"Our plans for today. The Doge's Palace. Lorenzo arranged a guided tour. We need to meet Paul Aiello in front of the palace at nine."

I lean towards Karen and whisper, "The guy who photographed this place and looks like a large shih tzu?"

Karen nods. Well, this could be interesting. We clean our plates and head upstairs to get ready. Moments later, we're weaving our way to St. Mark's Square. I scan the crowd. Costumed people dance as street musicians play or mill around, listening. Area cafes are filled with morning diners. No Paul or Dr. Virk, from what I can tell with all the costumes. I chuckle at the thought that if I whistle Paul would come running.

A thin man with a bad, mousy-brown combover wearing a gray polo shirt and khakis approaches Karen and me.

"*Signore y Signora* Novice, *sì?*"

"Yes," I reply hesitantly.

"I am Paul Aiello. Your guide." He searches our faces for recognition.

Karen looks him up and down. "I'm sorry, but you look very different from when you came to photograph Casa de Inglese."

"*Sì, sì*, that is my online blogger look."

Relieved, I extend my hand and shake his.

"Come now. I have the tickets to go in." He smiles and waves us toward the entrance. We follow him and step inside the palace.

"The *palaso* was built in 1340 in the Venetian Gothic style," Paul says. "It was the residence of the Doge of Venice, who was the supreme authority of the Republic of Venice. It has been destroyed by fire several times, rebuilt, and modified over the years. It became a museum in 1923."

We continue to make our way through the building with Paul giving facts and information regarding the palace, the interior, the artwork, and the uses of the building over the years. Paul has my interest when he speaks of the old prison cells and the Bridge of Sighs.

"The famous bridge was supposed to refer to the sighs of prisoners as they passed through the corridor, walking from the courtroom to the cell in which they would serve their sentence. The small windows allowed them one last look at the lagoon and sunlight."

We pause for a moment as a large tour group passes through. I'm looking out the window, contemplating what would have been going through a prisoner's mind, when I feel a presence next to me. I turn to meet a pair of dark, menacing eyes behind a blue-and-gold, jewel-encrusted mask. Their menace is equaled by the voice that accompanies them. "Stop pursuing me. France is behind us now. You have no business in my business. Make sure your wife stays safe."

Dr. Virk's words anger and concern me. Adrenaline shoots

through as I momentarily can't locate Karen. She's obscured by other tourists. In a panic, I push through the crowd until I see her chatting with Paul, totally unaware of the situation. When I look back, Dr. Virk has enveloped himself into the tour party and disappeared.

CHAPTER 7

Karen approaches me. "What's wrong?"

I grab her hand. "Dr. Virk was here and knows the police are interested in speaking with him."

Karen stares at me incredulously. "How does he know that? And that we'd be here today?" She swivels her head back and forth, scanning the crowd.

"I don't know, but we'll need to keep our eyes open in the future, especially with the crowds."

"Dan, people are wearing masks and costumes. He could be standing next to us and we may never know it. Do you think he knows where we're staying?"

"I hope not," I say with a shrug.

She rubs the top of my hand as reassurance. "I'm sorry I doubted you. Virk is here and serious. You're right. I'll be more aware of my surroundings."

I give her a half smile.

Paul, unsure of what we are talking about, glances between Karen and me. Karen waves it off. "Silly business from the past. Is there more to see?"

Paul continues through the palace. I don't hear what he's saying as I'm on high alert, swiveling my head from side to side and behind me, holding tight to Karen's hand. At the end of the tour, Paul bids us goodbye. Karen locks her arm in mine as we stroll through the streets. I feel completely drained, physically and emotionally, but still scan our surroundings when Karen abruptly stops.

"What?" I ask.

"I can't do this."

"Do what?"

She throws up her hands. "THIS! You, walking around at DEFCON 4." She takes a deep breath and slowly releases it. "I know we need to watch out for Dr. Virk, but we're on vacation in one of the most beautiful and romantic cities in the world. I want to enjoy it and think you're enjoying it."

I drop my shoulders. "I'm sorry. Dr. Virk is here and threatening you if I don't let what happened in France go."

"Then let it go. Caputo has the information and will do with it what he wants. I want to spend time here with my husband, not a cop," she snaps.

"I'm sorry. I'll try. Besides, there's a murder and robbery to look at." I shoot her a sideways glance. I'm not sure if she'll laugh or punch me. She chooses the latter.

My hand is then enveloped in hers. We weave and dodge our way to Il Sogno. Andrea is scurrying around tables, collecting plates and glassware as people finish their meals.

"A table for two," I ask, holding up two fingers.

He stops, but his eyes dart all around. "*Signore*, I am so sorry. We close for two hours after lunch to get ready for dinner."

"Not a problem," I say. "Maybe we'll come back later." Karen and I turn to leave.

He shouts after us, "No, no, you come!"

Karen shakes her head. "We're fine. It's okay."

"I insist. You come." Andrea motions for us to follow him inside the restaurant. Karen and I look at each other with bewilderment as he makes his way to the kitchen. He wipes off a place on the stainless-steel countertop and pulls two chairs beside it. Staff members swirl around, scrubbing pots and pans, wiping off surfaces, and filling a large dishwasher. Teresa is not there.

"*Lasciare*," Andrea orders. The staff look at us and leave the room. I guess he told them to go. He turns toward us, throwing open his arms. "Come, come. I will cook my best rigatoni for you. My 'treat,' as you Americans say." He places a pot of water on the stove, then begins mixing tomato sauce with cilantro, onions, salt, and a bit of grated cheese in a large pan. His watch alarm beeps.

"Do you need to be somewhere?" Karen asks.

"No, no. I have bad kidneys, but the medicine I take keeps me strong." He removes a small, round, plastic, blue case from his pocket and places pills in his mouth that he washes down with water.

"I'm sorry we're bothering you. This should be a time for you to relax," I say sympathetically.

"It is fine. I love to cook for people." When the pasta is ready, he adds it to the sauce, stirs, and plates it for Karen and me. "Eat."

It's the best I've ever tasted. Karen is humming with delight.

Andrea joins us at the counter.

"So, are you from Venice?" Karen asks him before biting a forkful of pasta.

Andrea shakes his head. "I come from a small village in the north. It is where my grandmother taught me to cook. This is her recipe."

"That's wonderful. We appreciate you sharing it with us," I say. "Do you like Venice?"

Andrea looks down as he rubs his fingertips on the counter. "Well, Venice is changing. More crime. Last night was very sad, but it has happened before."

My head pops up. "Before? Where before?"

He leans in. "Other places. Hotels, homes, even one of the mansions. When people are gone. Very bad."

"What are the police saying?" I ask.

"Not *polizia*. Lorenzo. He says that thieves must find out when people are gone. He thinks people put information on social media and the thieves see it."

I scratch my chin. "What does Lorenzo think of Anna's death at the costume shop?"

"He says that Mario did it, but that cannot be true. He was on a plane home from Spain. When he landed, he learned of his mother's death and went right there from the airport."

"Spain? What was he doing in Spain?" Karen inquires. I turn my head toward her and smirk. She rolls her eyes at me as she loads her fork.

"Mario works for a pharmaceutical company. He travels to many places as he trained as a chemist and speaks different languages."

I wonder whether or not he knows about poisons as I chew

another mouthful. The flavors of garlic, onion, and cilantro still dance in mouth.

Andrea begins to fidget in his chair. "Whoever did this is a bad person."

Karen and I scrape the small remains of our lunch and sigh with satisfaction. I stand and extend my hand. "Thank you so much. This was a special treat cooked by a master chef."

Andrea shakes my hand, beaming with pride. After saying goodbye, Karen and I wander out of the restaurant.

Several blocks later, I take Karen's arm. "Mario knows about drugs. He could've easily learned about poisons."

Mockingly, Karen replies, "I didn't think we were investigating Anna's death."

I stop and cross my arms over my chest. "Well, by now Caputo should have looked at the idea that Mario could have killed his mother. And, to tell you the truth, I'm not investigating, I'm exploring motives, and it was before we learned this information. He totally did it."

"He was on a plane coming home at the time," Karen snaps.

I wave my hand dismissively. "He could've arranged it before he left. Had someone drop the box of poisoned pins outside the shop while he was gone." I suck in a breath. "He and Katherine could be in it together, or Katherine thinks this is what he wants!"

"Okay, Sherlock, how are you going to prove it?"

"I don't know. I haven't gotten that far." I scratch my head. "I wonder if there were any fingerprints other than Katherine's on the box or wrapping. Is it too much to hope one or both would confess if Caputo asked them?"

"Yes, it is. I'm sure Caputo is checking for fingerprints, DNA, and stuff like that. Besides, we don't know Katherine was involved," Karen states, shaking her head. "Although she is hot after him. Even Arthur accused her of that. Motive! And she did bring the box into the store. I can't believe I'm saying this, but means and opportunity." She pauses before adding, "But Lorenzo was pretty quick to accuse Mario. I wonder why?"

"Lorenzo may think that Mario's in it for the money. His being able to sell the costume shop would give him lots of it."

"Or maybe there's something that happened between them that we don't know about. A Venetian vendetta."

I laugh out loud. "That's a bit melodramatic."

Karen chuckles. "Yeah, it was."

"Thanks for humoring me. Anna's death just bothers me," I say.

We link arms and meander along the Grand Canal.

Karen places her head on my shoulder. "You're a good man. That's why I love you."

I mull over what everyone has said or done. Murder, burglary, family angst. Who's involved? Who has something to gain? None of this is good.

Someone calling out catches my attention. I look down and see a gondolier. "*Bueno sera, signore e signora,*" he says.

"*Bueno sera* to you," I call back.

"You would like a ride?"

I look at Karen, who nods. We step into the gondola and pay for the ride.

"I am Tommaso," our gondolier states.

"This is Karen, and I'm Dan. Nice to meet you."

"I will give you a tour and tell you some history. You like ghost stories or no?"

Karen's nods, her curiosity piqued. "I love them."

"Good. Venice is full of love, death, murder, and spirits that roam among us." Tommaso chuckles. "I will tell them to you."

Karen snuggles into me.

Tommaso pushes the gondola from the pier. "You know of the two islands near Venice named Murano and Burano, *si*?"

We nod.

"The story is that in 1904, a great fog surrounded Venice. You could not see anything. A boat captain started to sail from Burano to take workers back home to Venice, but he did not know that two gondolas filled with passengers had started for Venice from Murano. The captain decided it was too danger-ous and turned back for Burano. The captain did not see the gondolas and ran into them. Five women disappeared into the water. Three bodies were found later, but two were not. The sister of one of the missing women said that she could smell roses. Her sister's favorite scent. Sofia came to her in a dream and said she was bound at the bottom of the canal and her sis-ter must pray for Sofia to be released. The sister prayed, and ten days later, Sofia's battered body appeared in the water, still wearing her lace dress with a red rose and a silver thread scarf around her neck. Rescuers say that she smelled of roses, even after being in the water."

"Did they ever find the other missing woman?" I ask.

Tommaso shakes his head. "No, never."

"That's so sad," Karen says.

"No, not really, *signora*. It is said that on foggy nights, Sofia appears along the canal as flickering silver lights to lead people to safety." Tommaso guides the boat through the calm water to an alleyway. "This is the back of the Venetian Opera House."

Karen sits upright. "That's so cool. Just like in the Donna Leon novel, *Death at La Fenice*."

"Okay, I guess I haven't read that one," I say, slightly confused.

"The book is set in Venice, and the main character is *Commissario* Brunetti. A death occurs at the opera house, and the author describes the police boat pulling up to the back of it. Now I'm seeing it."

Tommaso directs the gondola down various alleyways that reflect how people live their daily lives. Red geraniums in pots on windowsills, wash hung on clotheslines, and comforting smells of tomato sauce and cooked pasta lingering in the air. Tommaso pushes off a building to make a sharp right turn and return us to the pier.

I shake his hand. "That was wonderful. Thank you so much for the ride and the ghost story."

"I am glad you liked it," he replies. "*Arrivederci*."

Back along the canal, Karen and I stroll along, hand in hand.

"Do think that ghost story was true?" Karen asks me.

"You know I have a hard time believing in that, but it was fun to hear."

Lights flicker and sway on the water as shadows creep up between buildings and the sun bids another day goodbye.

Music and laughter rise from every direction as happy revelers scurry about. I take Karen's hand and swing her out. She twirls to the beat of the music and back to me. My knees don't appreciate some of the moves, but I don't care. This is where I want to be . . . with Karen. Half walking, half dancing, we arrive at Casa de Inglese, humming and laughing.

CHAPTER 8

Still humming, we enter the front hall. Loud, angry voices come from behind the closed library door, causing us to stop. I creep closer for a listen.

"Dan," Karen hisses, waving me toward the staircase.

I hold up my index finger. She rolls her eyes and shakes her head as she places her foot on the bottom step.

"Outrageous! How can you justify your actions?" bellows Arthur Ravencraft's voice.

The reply is too muffled to make out any words or the owner of the other voice. I lean closer to the door.

Arthur's voice is distinctly audible. "No more! You listen to me. As long as I'm in charge, I won't tolerate this behavior."

Fearing detection, I hurry to join Karen on the stairs. Arthur wrenches open the library door. Shock crosses his deeply red face when we make eye contact, but dissolves into a pressed smile.

"Sorry if you heard any of that, old boy. Stepdaughter not pulling her weight here at the family inn. Families, aye?" Arthur searches his jacket pockets for his pipe until he triumphantly pulls it out of an inner one. "There you are. Silly bugger."

I send him a brief wave while slowly continuing up the

stairs, hoping to see who he was speaking to. He looks around as if confused about where he's heading, then strides off toward the kitchen.

Behind our closed bedroom door, Karen turns to me. "What do you think that was about?"

I press a finger to my lips and point to the bathroom. Once there, I turn on the faucets to the sink and bathtub. "I don't know," I reply. "I was hoping to see who it was in the library with him, but didn't see anyone come out."

Karen sighs. "Well, we both know how difficult family relations can be, especially in a blended family. It's obvious that he and Katherine don't get along, and Harriet does criticize him. He could be trying to show he has some control in his life."

My phone buzzes with a text. "It's Lorenzo. He's meeting friends at a restaurant close by and wants us to join him. Mi Famiglia."

"I saw that place and wanted to eat there. Sounds like fun. Let's go," Karen replies.

After a short walk, we enter the dining room, which is dark and cramped, with far too many tables for the space. However, the warmth of the room and the rich aromas of freshly baked bread and tomato sauce make me want to sit and stay for a long time. The only customers appear to be Lorenzo and his group of eight men at the far corner. He sees us and waves us over. A couple of men stand and give us their seats, then pull over another table and chairs.

Lorenzo's voice loudly and happily greets us. "Good of you to come. Meet my friends here."

Names and handshakes follow, too many with heavy accents for me to catch each name. I do recognize Paul, our tour guide and blogger. Lorenzo elbows the man next to him. "Aldo, tell him what you said about the other thefts."

Aldo scans the room from side to side. "There have been more robberies in Venice over the past month. One was a couple that took a bus tour to Rome. It happened the first night they were gone, and their son found out the house had been broken into."

"I am not surprised it happened. They were telling everyone about their trip. You saw them at the *farmacia*." Lorenzo throws his hands up dramatically. "It was their first trip in a long time."

"My source tells me that he thinks the thieves watch people that are here for parties or post on social media and know when they are gone," Aldo adds.

"Are the thefts only happening during Carnival?" I ask.

Aldo nods. "Many. Not all."

I can't resist asking. "While we're talking about unsolved crimes, any more about the death of Anna?"

Lorenzo interrupts. "It was Mario. He wants money. This was his plan."

Aldo looks at the table.

"No, he would not do this," replies Paul. "I have known him for years. He loved his madre. It was the English lady from Casa de Inglese. She did it."

Karen asks, "Why would Katherine want to kill Anna?"

Paul looks between us with confusion. "No, no, not the young one. The old one."

"Harriet?" Karen and I chime in unison.

"*Sì*. Mario says she gives him many expensive gifts. She wants to sell everything and travel with him."

Karen and I look at each other with the same expression of total surprise. I want to explore the situation more when platters of bread and olive oil, sautéed vegetables, shrimp scampi, and spaghetti Bolognese arrive at the table with bottles of red and white wine.

Plates are passed, glasses filled, and conversation ceases for the moment. I can't believe I'm eating again, but it's too good to pass up.

Paul and Karen are talking about trying to find a day for a trip to the island of Murano to see the glass blowing factory and showroom. I'm still dwelling on the fact that Harriet and Katherine are interested in the same man. Did Anna not approve of either of them, or did Mario use one or both to help him kill his mother for the money from the sale of the shop?

"*Commissario* Caputo should know about Harriet and Katherine. He's investigating the death," I say to everyone.

Lorenzo looks up from his plate. "He knows," he grunts through a mouthful.

I mull over the list of suspects, now including Harriet. What is her connection to the murder, if any? She appeared unaffected the morning after the robbery at her own home. Does she know more about the crimes than she's telling? How do I approach Caputo to learn more about the direction the investigation is taking?

Lorenzo taps Karen's arm while the fork in his hand drops tomato sauce onto his shirt sleeve. Unphased, he says, "Arielle wanted me to ask you to come to her mother's funeral. It starts tomorrow afternoon. I will walk with you there. You too, Dan."

Karen cocks her head to one side. "I don't understand. Why us? It's very nice of her to ask, but she doesn't know us."

He waves his hand and empty fork dismissively. "In Italy, everyone is invited to the funeral. You are nothing special, but she said you were very nice to her after she found Anna. So, you will come." He turns his attention back to his plate.

Karen gives me a "what the heck" look. I shrug. I wonder if we both have something appropriate to wear. Personally, I hope to learn more about Anna's death.

The conversation turns toward soccer. I learn that one of the gentleman, Enzo, played for the national team, then became a sportswriter. A round of limoncello, a toast to the success of the team, is followed by more rounds to celebrate the team members, the coach, the hope for their rival Germany to lose, and some I forget. Karen stops at four rounds, but I finish mine and hers until I lose count. It's a night of laughter and companionship. Karen and I are now honorary supporters of Italian soccer.

Karen leans into me. "I'm way too drunk and need to go to bed."

It's late, but still feeling the warmth of the restaurant and newfound friendship, I reluctantly stand up, then lean on the table to steady myself as the full force of the drinks hits me. Smiling, with our arms linked together, Karen and I wave good night to everyone. We step out into the cold night air. She snuggles into me as we slowly walk to our bed-and-breakfast.

As we get nearer, I notice a silhouette near the front door. The person paces with something in his hand that glints when the light above the door catches it. I'm not sure if it's a weapon or something ordinary. My coppy senses start in, and I position Karen behind me. We continue toward the door, then realize it's Arthur Ravenscraft.

He looks up as we approach. "Hello, old man," he says. "I'm trying one of these new electric cigarettes but having a hard time with it. Harriet wants 'no more pipe smoke.'" He uses air quotes. "Rot, these silly things. Can't understand how my daft stepdaughter figured them out."

"May I see it?" I ask.

He hands me two pieces. I check both, gently reassemble it, and hand it back to him. "Try it now."

He draws a breath and puffs out pineapple-scented smoke, then slaps my back with a grin on his face. "Brillant. It works perfectly. Now, happy wife, happy life." He holds the door open for Karen and me to enter, then strolls toward the library.

Harriet comes from the kitchen, wiping her hands on a towel. "Arthur, put that silly thing away. You look like you're walking around with your own personal cloud encircling your head." She looks around. "What is that ghastly smell?"

He stands erect and proudly answers her question. "Pine-apple, my dear. Like my sea captain family members would bring home and place on their gate as a sign to welcome guests to visit their home."

"Such nonsense," Harriet snaps. "I prefer candles with subtle smells which give off the feeling this is a clean and wel-coming place. The smell of pineapple is not that. Put it away." She makes a quick spin on her heels and marches back toward the kitchen.

Arthur drops his head and shuffles to the library. So much for his thought of a happy wife.

Upstairs, I stumble a little in the doorway of our room. Karen looks back at me.

"Sorry, I think the doorway is swaying a little," I laugh. Karen snickers. I motion for her to join me in the bathroom with the faucets running.

"I don't want to upset you, and I'm not investigating. I'm just talking out loud."

Karen sighs. "I'm just drunk enough to play along."

"If Caputo knows about the love triangle of Mario, Harriet, and Katherine, then why haven't we seen him here interviewing them both?" I ask.

"Maybe he doesn't believe the rumor, or he's gathering more information from other sources before confronting them."

"I'm curious if he's spoken to Arielle about what she knows. You don't think she'd help her brother so they could split the sale of the shop, do you?"

"Dan, that's enough," Anger flares in her eyes. "Arielle is not involved in Anna's death. I'll bet my life on it." She changes clothes and the subject. "I need to get some sleep."

I let the conversation go, but my thoughts still run scenarios. I lie down next to Karen, who's deep, steady breaths have a relaxing effect on me. I drift off to sleep.

Karen screams, and I jolt awake, finding her sitting up in bed.

I'm propped up on my elbows, surveying the dark room. "What's wrong? Are you okay?"

She takes several slow, deep breaths. "I'm sorry. I was having this terrible dream. I was lost in a jungle, then I was walking on a tree-lined path. It was like *Alice in Wonderland*. The blue caterpillar character had Arthur's face. He wasn't smoking a hookah but had his e-cigarette. He kept calling me 'stupid girl' and trying to hand me his cigarette, but then it wasn't me, and I was watching the scene from a short distance. Another girl was there. He asked, 'Who are you?' The girl was about to answer, but then he lunged and thrust the cigarette at her. She fell backwards and laid there. I thought she was dead, so I screamed. That's when I woke up."

"Who was the girl?"

Karen shakes her head. "I can't be sure. I don't remember seeing her face, but I felt like I knew her."

Curiouser and curiouser that Karen's dream would have Arthur be assertive. I've not seen that displayed to this point. I pull her close to me, and we lie back down, hoping to still get some sleep.

CHAPTER 9

The sunshine through the curtains wakes me. I roll over, and Karen's gone. She steps out of the bathroom, dressed and ready for the day.

I look at her with concern. "You okay after last night's dream?"

"Yeah, thanks. Just a weird dream. I may have had a little too much to drink." She laughs. "But now I'm starving." That's my cue to get ready.

John and Linda are already seated as we step into the dining room. John waves us over, inviting us to sit down.

"It's good to see you both again. How are you doing?" Karen asks.

John throws up his hands. "Worried, but we're planning on staying in Venice."

Linda jumps in. "I'm sad about the robbery, but we've saved for so long for this trip, I want to try to enjoy it. I'm excited about tomorrow's formal ball."

Karen's face shows concern considering the robbery occurred during the last ball here.

Linda picks up on Karen's expression and pats her hand. "The thief won't come back to our room. We have nothing left to steal."

"I'm so sorry for you," Karen replies, her eyes empathetic. Linda nods.

Katherine enters the dining room and stops near our table with a deep frown on her face. "Oh . . . you're here. Did you want coffee or breakfast or something?"

Karen and I say, "Both," which apparently wasn't the right answer. Katherine audibly sighs and stomps to the kitchen. All four of us snicker at her response. Katherine returns with John and Linda's breakfast, but no coffee. Karen lets them know to eat while it's hot. Moments later, Harriet appears with a carafe of coffee and our breakfasts. She announces that the house will be closed from noon to 4:00 p.m. as her family will be attending Anna's funeral. I look at Harriet with a different perspective. Is she the murderer of her lover's mother who stood in her way to her freedom with him?

John and Linda are talking about their costumes for the formal ball.

"I hated that bloody plague doctor mask. I couldn't hear or see a thing," John states.

I'm relieved that there'll be one less plague doctor costume to suspect at the party.

"I also have another dress and hat," Linda says. "It's very different from my first one, but I want it to be a surprise. That nice girl at the shop helped me immensely, even after her mother's death."

"Arielle?" Karen asks Linda.

"That's her. Poor thing. I just feel so bad for her."

We finish eating and chat over a second cup of coffee until John and Linda excuse themselves. They state they're off to explore the island of Burano and the restored fishermen's cottages as well as doing a little shopping. Karen asks Linda to let her know what they think of the excursion.

After they leave, my phone rings. I answer it, have a short conversation, then turn to Karen. "That was Lorenzo. He will pick us up at one o'clock to go to Anna's funeral."

"Let's walk along the Grand Canal while we wait," Karen suggests to me. I take her hand as I reach for the door handle. The door flies open with no effort on my part and throws me off balance. A hand grabs my elbow to steady me. It's Caputo. He has a half smile on his face and humor in his eyes. "Steady on, old boy, as you Americans say."

Recovered, I reply, "That's the British . . . old boy." We shake hands. "Are you here to interview Katherine or Harriet? Or both?"

His eyes narrow as he searches my face for a tell of what I mean. "You know about them both?"

"I have my sources." I wink. "If you're interested, we can compare notes later."

The humor has left his eyes. "We can do that. Please join me at my office in an hour."

"Glad to," comes my reply.

Caputo continues further into the hall.

Karen looks at me. Her lips are set in a hard line. "Really?"

"What?" I say, giving it my best innocent voice. She slaps me on the back as she walks out the door. I hurry my pace to catch up with her.

"You're investigating . . . while on vacation . . . again!" Karen snaps.

"Oh, come on. Aren't you the least bit interested in who killed Anna?"

She rolls her head from side to side. "Okay, I'll admit, I'm a little interested. Just in the name of justice for Anna and Arielle."

I smile and nudge her elbow. "I knew you would."

She sighs. "The definition of insanity is doing the same thing over and over but expecting different results. We're on vacation, there's a murder of someone we know, you're investigating, and I expect a quiet trip. Yup, I'm insane."

"And I love you for it," I say with a big hug for her. "I'd kill to know what Caputo is asking Harriet and Katherine. Oh, sorry, poor choice of words."

Karen puts her hands on her hips. "No, you got it right. Come on, let's find some paper and pens so we can make notes." We pass a small gift shop and stop inside, where Karen finds a notebook and a pen with a small Venetian mask on its tip. I think she's more excited about finding the pen then actually working on the investigation. We make our way to one of the last remaining tables on the square at Caffè Florian, order two cappuccinos, and start. Each page in the notebook has a heading: suspects, motives, opportunity, access to the weapon, who benefits from Anna's death.

Karen writes the names of people on each list as we discuss them. Currently, the suspects include Mario, Arielle, Harriet, Katherine, and a yet unknown person. We review our findings to this point and discover that we can't eliminate any of our suspects. Mario was out of the country at the time of the murder, but his rumored involvement with both Katherine and

Harriet could mean he used them to his own end. Katherine carried the box of poisoned pins into the shop, so her fingerprints would be on the outside of the box, but will anyone else's? That's one of my questions for Caputo if he's willing to share.

It's time to meet Caputo at his office. I stand up and extend my hand to help Karen. She takes my hand and nearly pulls me over.

"Oh, no!" she exclaims, staring into the crowd.

I swivel my head back and forth. "What?"

"Dan, you're right. Dr. Virk is here in Venice *and* he's holding hands with Katherine."

"Where?" I scan faces in the area but can't locate either Dr. Virk or Katherine.

"They've disappeared into the crowd. They were sitting at a table over there." She waves her index finger toward the café, then turns to me with fear in her eyes. "How would he know Katherine?"

I shake my head. Did he follow us to the bed-and-breakfast and make friends with Katherine to keep track of us? Does he have more sinister plans? Is he involved in the thefts or Anna's death? Plots are spinning in my mind.

Karen taps my arm. "We need to talk to Caputo. If he questions Katherine, he may have learned the name Virk is using here in Venice."

I doubt it. If he has plans here, he'll have lied about his name or changed it since arriving.

The walk to the police station has me fraught with anxiety. Too many people around us, masked and unidentifiable.

The station is just as chaotic. A cacophony of voices, officers moving about, people in different levels of distress, reporting everything from picked pockets to assaults. One guy sits on a wooden bench with paper towel to his bloody nose. I approach the desk and ask the officer seated there for Caputo. He dials the desk phone. Moments later, Caputo waves us through the locked lobby door into the squad room. He leads us to his office, closing the door behind us.

Caputo directs us to two wooden chairs in front of his black painted wood desk. He positions himself behind it in a high-back, brown leather chair, then leans forward, elbows on the desk, fingertips pressed together. "So, what can you tell me about Harriet Ravenscraft and Katherine Oldman?"

I relay what I learned from Paul Aiello, that Mario had talked about being involved with Harriet. I added that Arthur Ravenscraft had accused Katherine of pursuing Mario. Caputo listens. His eyes and body language give no indication as to whether he is aware of the situation or not, so I ask.

Caputo smiles weakly. "I did know some, and discovered some."

An answer that reveals nothing. That's what I would do. I like this guy.

"Are you any closer to naming a suspect?" I inquire.

"Not at this time. We are still gathering evidence. Rumor has little place in an investigation."

Karen explains her sighting of Dr. Virk and Katherine. She suggests that Katherine may know the name Virk is using at this time.

Caputo acknowledges her information. "I'll ask her about it."

I pull my chair closer to the desk. "Any prints on the package of poisoned pins?"

He looks at me, rubbing the thumb of his left hand across his fingers, then averts his eyes. I'm frozen in place, waiting for him to decide to trust me.

When his gaze comes up again, he answers, "Nothing but what we expected. Katherine's and Arielle's were on the wrapping. Anna's on the box."

"Were you able to trace where the package was sent from?"

He relaxes his shoulders. "No. There was no shipping information." He leans back in his chair. "It appears that someone hand-carried the package. We are viewing nearby surveillance video, but Carnival is busy day and night. It may be impossible to find the person that left the box."

"Anything more about the robbery at the bed-and-breakfast?" Karen asks.

Caputo shakes his head. "Nothing has been reported at any of the shops. However, with so many people leaving Venice daily, the items may already be out of Italy." He stands up. "I'm sorry. Thank you for coming."

I can't read his expression, but that's our cue to leave. We head back to get ready for the funeral. Karen changes into a simple knee-length black dress with long sheer sleeves. I wear black pants, a white, long-sleeved dress shirt, and a burgundy tie. We head down to the lobby.

Lorenzo is waiting. "Come, we go." Once outside, he weaves through the crowd to a Catholic church on a side alley. It's three buildings with sloping sides, built of red brick and accented with white plaster columns. The center building boasts a large rose window with a wooden double-door entrance and a white stone pointed arch over it. This is a neighborhood church, not a giant cathedral. It feels right for Anna, whose life was here.

Inside is dark and cool. An overwhelming smell of flowers saturates the air. In front of the altar and down the side aisles are nearly thirty arrangements in various sizes. A large number of people occupy pews, some sitting and others kneeling in prayer. Arielle and Mario are near the casket at the front of the church. Lorenzo walks past the line of mourners waiting to speak with Arielle and Mario and goes straight to Arielle. "Dan, Karen, follow me."

Karen leans into me and whispers, "I guess he doesn't wait in line." I'm uncomfortable moving past others, but Lorenzo waves us to him.

Karen and I give Arielle and Mario our condolences. Both accept them graciously. Lorenzo pushes past me and back down the aisle. "We find a place to sit." When the organ begins to play, Arielle and Mario sit as the rest of the crowd enters the rows of wooden pews.

Lorenzo positions himself near the front of the church while Karen and I sit in the row behind him. The funeral service starts. A priest and four altar boys enter from the back of the church. It's beautiful to listen without understanding a word. Karen and I follow along with the crowd when it's time to stand, sit, or kneel.

When the service is over, Lorenzo turns to me. "There is food downstairs. We will eat now."

The church hall is crowded with people and platters, bowls,

and slow cookers of amazing Italian food. Lorenzo hands Karen and me each a plate. "Eat." He takes a plate for himself and starts filling it, so Karen and I join in. Plates full, we find a couple of seats at the far end of the room. I look for the men's room. Across the room, I head down a small hall with a door at the end, hoping this is it. I wrap my fingers around the door handle just as I hear something.

"Get your hands off me!" Dani's voice shrieks.

Malice and venom saturate Arthur's voice. "You listen here. Do as you're told. You will not ruin this for me. If you try, you'll be sorry."

"You don't frighten me, il vecchio. Enough," Dani spits back. The door flies open, and Dani steps back in surprise when she sees me. She straightsens her blouse, tucking it in as she pushes past.

I step into the doorframe, blocking Arthur's escape. "What's going on here?"

Arthur sputters, "Nothing, old man. Stupid girls always get the wrong idea. Must be off." He takes a step forward, but I fail to relinquish the right of way.

"It doesn't sound like nothing or that Dani was being stupid. It sounded like you were threatening her. Why?" I demand.

"She's troubled. Blackmail." He waves a chubby finger in my face with emphasis. "She said that she'd tell Harriet I was 'at it' with her unless I paid. I love my wife and don't want it ruined by a lie. That girl has ideas above her station. Doesn't want to work behind the counter at the pharmacy. Her parents built that business up and just gave it to her. She wants to sell it and run away with Mario after he sells his mother's shop."

I'm shocked. Another woman thinks she'll have a life with Mario and the money he thinks he'll have? How many are there? Did Dani help kill Anna?

Arthur pushes past me, nearly knocking Karen over.

"Is everything okay?" she asks. "You were gone awhile, then I saw Dani run out. Arthur looks angry. I hope nothing's wrong."

I throw up my hands. "We have another suspect to add to our list. I'll tell you more when we're back in our room. Let's eat."

CHAPTER 10

Karen crinkles her forehead but doesn't ask any more questions. I'm running scenarios through my head, adding a name to the suspect list and making a note to contact Caputo about what I heard and experienced. We sit back down and finish our plates of food in silence.

The noise level is high. People in small groups talk, laugh, and slap each other on the back. I don't understand the words. The smells of tomato sauce and cooked pasta linger in the air, causing the room to feel warm and cozy. Several volunteers are picking up abandoned cups, plates with remnants of food, crumbled napkins, and plastic utensils that litter tables, then are wiping off each table. Arthur sits at a table with Harriet, who is picking at items on her plate. They aren't speaking or even looking at each other. Harriet is staring at the door. Hoping to flee, or maybe see Mario? Arthur's glaring at Dani, who's sitting at another table with Katherine. Their heads are close together, and Katherine is rubbing Dani's back. Neither looks at Arthur.

I snicker to myself when I realize what this is. Mario in the center of all the women's circles. They overlap and intertwine with each other.

Karen nudges my arm. "What's so funny?"

"I'll show you later." I lean back in my chair and scan the scene being played out . . . in a church hall, of all places. Mario enters the room, and all eyes focus on him. Harriet pulls herself up more erectly as he crosses the room. Arthur is keenly aware of his wife's interest. Katherine gives a smile and a wave in Mario's direction. His eyes sweep the room, then he makes his way to a group of men and stands with his back to everyone else. Harriet's face hardens, and her jaw clenches. Katherine slumps her shoulders forward, dropping her hand into her lap, her smile replaced by sadness. Dani leans in to talk to her. Katherine nods while wiping tears from her cheeks. Harriet stands and walks to the exit, leaving Arthur sitting alone at the table. He pulls his e-cigarette from his inside jacket pocket and shuffles toward the door, a trail of smoke hanging in the air in his wake. Several people look after him with disdain. What roles do Arthur and Harriet play in this drama? Is their marriage as tumultuous as they make it appear?

Lorenzo stops at our table. "I am going with friends. You know your way back to the inn, *si*?"

Karen smiles up at him. "We'll be fine. It's a nice night for a walk."

He smacks his hand on the table triumphantly and returns to his group.

"Are you ready?" Karen asks.

"Yeah, I think so. Can't decide if I want more to eat or not, but I'm loving the in-house entertainment."

"You mean the love triangle with Mario? Or more like a square or pentagon."

"You saw it too?"

She laughs. "It's a good thing looks can't kill. When he ignored Harriet, I was waiting for laser beams to shoot out of her eyes into the back of his head."

Curiouser and curiouser.

Once outside, the air is refreshingly cool, damp, and crisp. I notice we're nearly alone on the street. No tourists or partygoers. This is where residents live their daily lives. Karen wraps her arm around mine as we stroll down a long, winding street.

Once we reach a corner, I stop. I'm not quite sure which way we came. It all looks different going back.

Karen looks at me. "Are we lost?"

"Maybe? No, wait. I remember the sign for the dentist's office on this corner as we came this way. After that, it may be a little difficult."

At the corner, I'm right. We look in each direction, but nothing is familiar.

"Well, I'll follow you," Karen says. "You're the one who passed orienteering in the Army."

"Let's turn left. If we can find a hotel, they may have staff that speak English or have a map. Right now, we're in a cellular dead zone."

We start walking. The light is fading, and fog has descended. The alleyways take on an ominous look. If we can make our way to the Grand Canal, we'll know where we are. However, Venice is a maze of alleys, bridges, and passageways that wind between rows of buildings. They're eerily quiet and void of people. We stop at each intersection to look for familiar landmarks, but we're disappointed time and time again.

"Dan, I think we need to stop and ask someone for directions to St. Mark's Square, then we'd know how to get home."

We continue until we see a figure slowly walking in the distance. Karen approaches the woman, who's wearing a full-length black lace dress and veil. "*Signora, mi scusi*. Piazza San Marco?"

I can't hear a response, but a crooked finger points down the alley.

"*Grazie*," Karen says. She joins me. "I don't think she spoke English. Let's go the way she pointed." When we look back, the woman is gone, but a whiff of roses floats in the air. After a block or so, I swear I hear footsteps behind us, and I grab Karen's arm. We stop, and so do the footsteps. I shake my head; maybe I didn't hear them. We start again, and so do the footsteps. Someone is behind us.

"Let's hurry," I whisper to Karen.

We quicken our pace, and the footsteps speed up. The next corner brings us to the Grand Canal. I can see the outline of the Doge's Palace a few feet in front of me. I know where we are now and turn for the inn. A crowd of merrymakers in costume walk directly at us, bringing forth a sigh of relief from me. All is back to normal. I pull Karen against a building to allow them to pass. Once they've passed, the footsteps return. I step away from the building to determine who may be coming our way. At the end of the block, a figure obscured in the fog stops when they see me. I can't tell if it's a man or a woman. As they raise something above their head, I step forward to confront them but spin around when a hand touches my back. I'm face-to-face with Caputo.

"Is something wrong?" he asks.

I release a deep breath. "I can't be sure. I thought someone was following us." When I look back, the figure is gone. A distinctive splash comes from the canal, as if something heavy was just thrown in. "What are you doing here?"

He sets his mouth in a hard line. "There was another robbery at another bed-and-breakfast. I'm on my way to investigate. Go home. Get out of this damp air."

"Thanks, we will," I say. Caputo waves goodbye and disappears into the fog. I hold Karen's hand as we move toward home.

Suddenly Arthur is alongside me. My coppy senses kick in. I sweep Karen behind me and confront him. "Where did you come from?"

"I-I . . . the church, old boy," he utters, his eyes wide with confusion at my question.

I take a step toward him. "Were you following us this whole time?"

"Steady on. I wasn't. I got turned around in this bloody fog. Can't see a thing."

Karen and I look after him as he moves in the direction of his bed-and-breakfast. We wait a few moments before starting out again.

A line of lights can be seen flickering in the water on the edge of the canal, even through the fog. Calm washes over me as a strong smell of roses hits my nose.

"Do you smell that, Dan? Sofia is watching over us. We're safe."

The entrance to the bed-and-breakfast smells of pineapple.

Arthur made it home. The lobby feels warm and bright after the gloom from the outside. Karen and I trudge up the stairs to our room and close the door behind us.

Karen pauses at the doorway.

"What is it?"

"We should check that nothing is missing or out of place."

A thorough search reveals nothing amiss. Karen takes a long, hot bath to get rid of the evening chill. I move a chair in front of the bedroom door and check that the French doors are secure, using one of my long-sleeve T-shirts to tie the doors together.

Once we're both in bed, we spend the rest of the evening reading. I must have fallen asleep because someone is shaking me, calling me to wake up. "Dan! Wake up!" Karen urges. I think I hear someone screaming, but that must still be my dream.

Her shaking persists. "Dan . . . Dan! Wake up!"

I sit up and face Karen, willing my eyes to focus, but the room is dark. "Why? What's wrong?"

"Someone is screaming."

Someone *is* screaming. The clock reads 11:30 p.m. Was that another scream? I throw off the covers, get dressed, and grab my phone. My mind is racing to figure out what's happening. Karen's right behind me as we step out into the hallway.

"Help me!" wails down the hall. We move in that direction. At the end of the hall, Harriet is standing outside the open door of one of the guest rooms, looking in, shaking and crying. "Help her, please," she implores as we approach. I step around Harriet and into the room. There's a body on the floor. I use my shirt sleeve to turn the light on. It's Katherine.

"She complained of a headache when she came home from the church, so she went into her room to lie down," Harriet says. "I was bringing her a cup of tea when I found her like this. Please, help her." Her body shudders as she sobs.

An overturned teacup rests on the floor near Katherine's hand. I check her wrist. Her body is still warm, but no pulse. Her eyes are open and fixed. "I'm sorry, there's nothing that can be done. She's dead," I say sympathetically.

Harriet doubles over, crying and rocking her body.

I turn to Karen. "Call Caputo. I have his number in my contacts. I'll send it to you."

She nods. "Be careful. I smell bitter almonds." She maneuvers Harriet back to our room while I survey the scene. Katherine is sprawled on the floor, eyes open, skin pink-tinged, hair twisted, and hands clenched. A small pool of vomit lies on the floor next to her. Did she have a seizure? Her e-cigarette is still in her right hand. If Karen's right, then the e-cigarette could contain cyanide.

Karen briefly returns. "Caputo's on his way. I'll stay with Harriet."

I take photos of the body, the room in general, items in plain sight, the dropped teacup, and the cigarette.

Wheezing in the hall causes me to back up to the door-frame. Arthur's leaning over, clutching the wall and gasping for breath. He raises his head. "What's the meaning of this? What's happened here?"

I explain the situation, that Harriet is with Karen and the police have been called. He tries to push his way into the room.

I plant my feet, firmly blocking his path. "You need to stay out of this room. Please go downstairs to wait for the police. Let them know the situation is up here."

"This . . . this . . . situation . . . such rot. Now this is in my house," Arthur mutters as he turns down the hall. His footfalls are heavy on the stairs.

I step back into the room. A hairbrush, makeup, and nail polish are strewn on top of Katherine's dresser. Her clothes are everywhere—some hung up, with additional piles on the floor and bed. But no jewelry is visible. Did she surprise the thief? If she was poisoned, that takes planning ahead of time, not a spur-of-the-moment killing.

Pulling fingerprints from this room will be a nightmare. Eliminating them will be even worse. Who wants this girl dead? Mario? Arthur? Dani? I doubt Harriet would.

Raised voices from downstairs capture my attention, so I step back into the hall. Two uniformed officers round the corner at the top of the stairs. One has dark hair, the other has lighter, curly hair, and both are young. One gives commands in Italian.

I put my hands up. "*No italiano.*" I'm not sure if that's correct, but he gets the message.

"Please step back," he snaps, his eyes dark and serious. I slowly move away from the doorway. He signals to his partner, then points to me. I translate that to mean "cover him" while the first officer peers into the room. The radio on his belt crackles with words I don't understand, but I hope Caputo is on his way.

My legs are starting to hurt from standing in the hall. I let the officer know that I'm going to my room to sit down.

He glares at me. "No, you stay."

Should I ignore him? Before I can decide, Caputo steps into view. He waves the officer off and proceeds to inspect the scene before turning to me. "Did you discover the body?"

I shake my head and explain how I came to be there. I mention that Harriet was distraught, and Karen is looking after her in our room.

He turns back to the room, pulling gloves out of his back pocket, and retrieves the e-cigarette.

"Careful," I say. "My wife swears she could smell burnt almonds or cyanide."

He cocks his head to look at me and smiles. "I too smell it."

"Really? I can't smell it at all," I admit.

Thundering footsteps on the stairs indicate that the other officers have arrived, carrying crime scene gear. The five-person team begins processing the scene.

Caputo takes my elbow and guides me toward my room. "Did you question Harriet or Arthur at all?"

"No, I didn't. She was overwhelmed with grief, and I directed Arthur to wait for the police downstairs to get him out of the way. I waited for your people to show up."

We arrive at my room. Inside, Harriet is sobbing, a pile of shredded tissue resting on the bed. Karen sits next to her.

"Would you two excuse us, please?" Caputo asks firmly, showing us the way out. Karen and I silently leave, closing the door behind us.

CHAPTER 11

Karen whispers to me, "Who do you think did this?"

"Both victims, Anna and Katherine, are associated with many of the same people. Mario, Dani, Harriet, Arthur, Lorenzo," I reply.

A deep furrow appears on Karen's forehead. "Lorenzo? What would he gain by killing both people?"

"I don't know. They're just so intertwined." I rub my fingers on my temples. "There's something we're missing, or else two random murders took place in the same group of people. I don't believe in coincidences."

Karen hugs me. "Mario I could see, but Dani was Katherine's friend, and Harriet was her mother. She didn't like her stepfather. Did Arthur do it to get her out of the way?"

I plan to ask Caputo if Harriet has a will and who would benefit, Katherine or Arthur. With Katherine gone, does he stand a better chance to inherit?

Caputo opens the bedroom door. Harriet leans on him as they start for the staircase, her composure regained, but she stares forward vacantly.

"Please join us downstairs," Caputo tells Karen and me. "I'll need to interview everyone that was in the house."

"We'll be down shortly," Karen quietly replies.

We head back into our room and finish dressing before going down. The door to the library is closed when we arrive.

Arthur is pacing the hall, puffing his pipe and muttering, "No respect. This will never do. My house. Deserve respect."

Karen and I move closer to the kitchen, but he catches sight of us. I cringe.

He bellows across the hall, "Impertinent, that's what this is! That girl is nothing but a problem. She has to go and die here. What will people think? The police here . . . this will never do."

I'm taken aback at his coldness toward his stepdaughter. Bad relationship or not, she's been murdered.

The library door opens. Harriet steps out, followed by Caputo.

Arthur stomps right up to Caputo. "I demand to be kept informed of the proceedings."

Caputo's eyes flash with anger.

Harriet snaps her head toward Arthur. Her eyes flare. "You're not in charge here."

He withers under her gaze. "Yes . . . yes, my dear. As you say. Can I get you something to help with the shock you've had?"

"To be left alone" comes the toxic response. Arthur drops his head and steps back from her. Caputo watches the scene without any expression.

Harriet's face transforms to a soft hue as she turns to Karen and me. "I'll have coffee ready in a few minutes."

Karen looks between me and Harriet. "That's not necessary. It's been a terrible loss for you. We're fine."

"I insist. This is *MY* bed-and-breakfast," Harriet says as she spins on her heels and heads for the kitchen.

Caputo shows Arthur into the library and closes the door. While Karen and I remain in the hall, I think back on what I know about the victim. She had a poor relationship with her stepfather, but that's not unheard of. Karen saw her with Dr. Virk earlier today. I can't help but believe he's involved in this situation somehow. Then, of course, there's Mario. Did she kill his mother and he retaliated, or did she know too much about Anna's death and become a liability? I place Harriet further down my suspect list but won't eliminate her. She may be a colder personality, but I doubt she'd kill her daughter, unless Katherine threatened Harriet's future happiness with Mario.

Arthur turns back toward the library to address Caputo. "Very good, my man. Keep me informed. I'd hate to have to go to your superior officers." Arthur puts his pipe in his mouth and hums on his way to the kitchen.

Karen and I join Caputo in the library. He sits behind the desk, dark stubble on his face, and we fill the slim wooden chairs in front of it, then retell our participation in the situation. He writes something in a brown leather-bound notebook.

When we finish our account, he leans back in the chair. "I'd like you to assist me in this case, unofficially, of course. No one else needs to know. You seem to have gained the trust of people involved that I can't. Is it a deal?"

I jump up and extend my hand. He shakes it.

"Karen and I have some notes about what we've observed. I'd like to share them with you."

A deep sigh escapes from Karen. I try to contain my excitement at investigating but can't repress the smile on my face.

"If you two detectives don't need me, I'm going back to

bed," Karen says, standing up and administering a gentle slap to the back of my head. She opens the door and steps aside as Harriet brings in a tray of coffee, cups, and muffins. Harriet places the tray on the desk, then breezes out as if there weren't a care in the world. I wonder about the British "stiff upper lip."

Karen's on the stairs when I catch up with her. "Don't say a word," she warns. "I knew you'd end up being part of the investigation."

"You're right. Sorry, but I need to do this. I'll just grab the notes we started and show them to Caputo. Don't wait up."

Her response is a simple roll of her eyes.

Back in the library, Caputo and I discuss the group of men at Mi Famiglia.

"From my talking with them, it appears that one or more have information that when put together could be a lead in the murders and possibly the burglaries."

With his fingertips pressed together, Caputo listens. He's aware of many of the men I speak of.

"Would you be able to meet with them again and learn what other information they may have?" he asks.

I agree, but I'm not sure Karen will. I pour each of us a cup of coffee. Caputo waves off a muffin, but I take a bite of a chocolate one. I surprise myself that, again, I'm hungry.

"I know it sounds like I'm not on the same subject, but Katherine was with Dr. Virk. What if she learned something she shouldn't have, like his real name, or maybe the name he's using in Italy? He knows that I've reported him to you. If he thought she'd turn him in, I believe he'd kill her to stop that from happening."

Caputo looks up. "Well, it's too late to ask her what she knows about him. If he did kill her, we'll have to find him another way."

He asks about other guests staying here. I inform him of John and Linda, the burglary victims, and realize they didn't appear when Harriet was screaming for help, or when the police arrived.

"I'll follow up with them later." He excuses himself to check on how the crime scene techs are doing. I'm right behind him up the stairs, where a flood of Italian is being spoken. I attempt to look inside the room while they work, but a uniformed officer waves me to back up.

I head for my room. Karen's in bed, breathing deeply. I slide in as stealthily as possible and fall asleep with no effort.

Karen jumps awake, her movement waking me up as well.

"You okay? Bad dream?" I groggily ask.

She nods. "I'm sorry. I was dreaming I was in an enclosure with high fences, and I was locked in, but when I tried to climb to the top, someone pushed me, and I fell."

"Did you see who it was?"

"No, but I feel like it was a man and I know him somehow."

We snuggle back down until sunshine through the curtains and a glance at the clock show me it's late morning. "I think we missed breakfast."

"We can walk for something. I just feel off schedule," Karen replies. "I'm going to get up and start the day."

"I'll bet ready when you're done." I lie back on my pillow with a slight headache. I'm sure I'm a few cups short of caffeine. Once Karen is back, showered and dressed, and I get ready, we head out the bedroom door. The crime scene techs are gone, but the police tape remains on the door. A pang of sadness hits me for the loss and the fact that it was an unexpected death. Karen glances at the tape but doesn't comment. At the top of the stairs, we see John and Linda coming up from the lobby.

"You missed breakfast," John says, extending his hand. I shake it.

I glance at John, not sure if he's aware of what happened. "Well, the excitement early this morning got us off track."

Confusion crosses his face. "Excitement? What do you mean?"

"Katherine's been found dead in her room," I explain. Wide-eyed, their mouths hanging open, John and Linda stare at me in shock. John runs his hand over his head. Linda is shaking slightly.

"You didn't hear anything at all?" Karen asks.

A surprised look crosses John's face. "We weren't here, mate. Linda and I had such a great time on Burano yesterday that we stayed over. Took the first ferry back and made it in time for breakfast."

Linda wrings her hands.

Karen looks at her. "Are you okay?"

"No!" Linda snaps back. "There's something wrong with this place. First, we're robbed, and now a death. I'm afraid to sleep here. What if John and I are next?" John reaches for Linda's arm, but she yanks it away. "Stop. I'm serious. If this trip didn't cost so much, I'd tell you we're going home."

Her facial expression is hard to read. She'll either cry or punch something. She starts for her room.

"*Commissario* Caputo will be here later to interview you both," I say.

Linda turns and faces me. "Why?" she shouts. "We don't know anything. We weren't even here last night."

I lean forward. "But you both knew the victim. There may be something, even trivial, that may help."

Linda's eyes focus on the floor, and her voice softens. "You're right. I'm sorry I snapped at you. This is very stressful." She heads up the stairs. John pats my shoulder as he passes.

Karen and I make our way down the stairs and through the hall to the outside. The breeze is cool but so much fresher than the oppressive air inside. We walk for several blocks until we see Il Sogno. Several people in costume sit at the outdoor tables, conversations and laughter carrying through the air. I scan the area for an open table.

"Paul Aiello is sitting at one of the tables," Karen states. He's looking at his phone, sipping a cappuccino, when we approach him.

"May we join you?" Karen asks.

He's startled but motions for us to sit down. Karen questions if a tour of the Murano Glass Factory can happen in the next day or two.

"I will make a call. One minute," Paul says as he dials his phone. Italian flows back and forth until he hangs up, smiling at us. "*Signora* is in luck. We can go for a tour tomorrow morning."

Karen beams. "Thank you. That's wonderful."

A young curvaceous woman with dark hair pulled into a bun at the top of her head and soft brown eyes approaches our table. "You would like a coffee or cappuccino?"

Paul waves his arm above his head at her. "Amata, yes, bring them each a coffee, *sì*?" Karen and I nod.

Amata smiles and walks toward the kitchen.

Karen leans into Paul and whispers, "Who's that? I haven't seen her before. Is she new?"

He frowns at Karen. "No, no, Amata has worked here a long time. She is a good friend of Teresa. She went on vacation to, I think, New York City recently."

It seems odd that during the busiest time of the year she would be allowed vacation time, but I'm not her boss. I turn the conversation to an invitation to gather the group together for another evening at Mi Famiglia.

A smile creeps across Paul's lips. "*Sì*, we are all interested in the death at the casa." He pushes his cup to one side and leans forward on the table. "Did the police talk to you? Do they know what happened?"

I shrug nonchalantly. "They interviewed Karen and I because we were in the house when it happened."

Paul looks around and lowers his voice. "Do you think that Caputo will talk to you because you are a detective? Lorenzo says that Katherine surprised the thief and he had to kill her, if she knew him."

"Why would the thief be in Katherine's room?" I ask.

"Lorenzo says she spent all her money on jewelry. Do you know how she died? If she was strangled and killed with a knife, then Lorenzo could be right."

"I think the police are working on when and how she died," I reply as Amata places our coffees on the table.

I know Lorenzo's scenario won't work. It was not a spontaneous murder. However, if Katherine threatened to blackmail the thief or reveal their identity, a poisoned e-cigarette may just work as a murder weapon. The killer could have a solid alibi for the time of her death. She was alone in her room. No sign of a struggle with anyone.

CHAPTER 12

Amata takes our lunch order. Paul declines anything to eat and instead speaks Italian into his phone. I catch words like "*Mi Famiglia*" and "*cena*," which I think means "dinner." Tables around us quickly fill up with a visual parade of colored costumes and masks. Many languages surround us, and I feel my anxiety rising. Karen looks at me and winks. She knows it's just too busy for my comfort.

Lunch arrives. Karen has spaghetti Bolognese and I have linguini by the sea. We tuck into them as Paul places his phone on the table.

"I have made reservations for tonight at 8:30," Paul states. "I have called a few people, so we will see who comes."

I nod, as my mouth is full of food, then swallow. "Thank you for doing all that. I look forward to tonight."

Paul stands and excuses himself. "I will see you tonight." He heads off into the crowd. Karen and I finish our lunches, pay our bill with Amata, and wave to Andrea as he scurries around, clearing tables.

"I feel better now that I've eaten, but it was an early lunch," Karen says, laughing. "I feel dishonest about what we're doing tonight at Mi Famiglia. We're acting like spies for Caputo and the investigation. Or at least you are."

"Not really. Paul said that the members of the group are interested in Katherine's death. I'd like to talk to Caputo today and find out what I can share, then see what I learn from the group. Information is going both ways."

Karen shoots me a sideways glance to let me know she's not convinced that's what's happening, then switches gears, happily chatting about our trip to Murano. "I want to *investigate* finding a glass-blown ornament for our vacation tree." She decorates a tree each Christmas with ornaments from places we've traveled. Each is a great memory.

My phone chimes. "It's Caputo," I say. "He wants me to stop by his office. He has something. Would you like to join me?"

She sighs. "Fine."

"Five minutes, maybe ten . . . no more than twenty minutes, I promise," I say.

Her laser-focused, unyielding eyes impart her disbelief in my statement. I snicker as she's right . . . it'll take longer.

We traverse through the crowds and performers of the plaza on our way to the police station. Caputo's at the door when we arrive, lets us in, and leads the way to his office.

The door closed behind him, we all sit down. He shuffles through a mass of white paper until he finds what he's looking for. "The autopsy report confirms that Katherine died of cyanide inhaled from her e-cigarette. Trace amounts were found in the cartridge. A search of her room turned up a variety of cartridges and cartomizers. More than one was tainted. The unused ones were in an unlocked drawer, and tests discovered several, including those flavors labeled coffee, pineapple, menthol, and chocolate. The last one used was cappuccino-flavored.

"If the smell and taste of the cappuccino was strong enough, it could've masked the bitter almond scent," Karen states, looking at me and Caputo.

I lean forward and rest my elbows on the desk. "I can't smell cyanide. Maybe she couldn't either. The first draw on the cigarette would be all it takes."

As I look back at Caputo, his eyes lose all humor. "I need to ask, Dan, why the e-cigarette, which is the murder weapon, would have a print from you?"

My mind whirls with disbelief. I know I didn't touch the cigarette when the body was found, and I don't remember handling her cigarettes any other time. "I have one explanation. Could she and Arthur have exchanged or mixed up cigarettes? I helped him assemble his."

A sly smile crosses Caputo's lips. "*Sì*, I have questioned Arthur about Katherine's smoking. He and Katherine ordered the same model. Many times, they mixed up each other's. Prints from Katherine and Arthur were also found; however, there were no prints on any of the remaining cartridges. Harriet had insisted that Katherine give up tobacco and Arthur his pipe, but then wasn't happy with the smell of smoke from the e-cigarette either."

A deep *whew* escapes my lips. "I was afraid I was a suspect there for a moment."

Karen pats my shoulder. "So did I."

"You were," Caputo remarks dryly. "I'm not ruling anyone

out . . . not yet. A search found that both Katherine and Arthur had the same cartridges and flavors. Arthur said he's gone back to his pipe but smokes it more discreetly as Harriet does not like it."

"Do you know when the items were ordered?" Karen asks.

"Katherine placed the order for everything two weeks ago. It would have been possible to tamper with the cartridges at any time since they arrived. They were not kept locked up. Casa de Inglese is not a very secure inn."

Karen and I agree, given the recent burglary. We turn our attention to Caputo's incident board as he lifts the sheet to reveal it. Two separate murder investigations are there. Karen looks at me with surprise as both of our pictures are listed for Katherine's death.

"I see we haven't been eliminated from your inquires," I remark with sarcasm.

Caputo shrugs. "No one has. Anyone in the house or known to either victim is there. Only solid evidence will determine who stays up there."

"We're off the hook for Anna's murder," I say.

He furrows his brow. "What does 'off the hook' mean?"

I laugh out loud. "Sorry. It refers to a fish that manages to get 'off the hook' and escape capture." I emphasize with finger quotes. "I'm saying that neither Karen nor I could be involved as we entered the shop after Anna was dead."

"True. I don't really suspect you of Katherine's murder. However, you were at both scenes when the bodies were discovered," he says to me, his eyebrows raised.

I don't have a good response to that statement. "Sorry?"

He waves dismissively at me. I'm happy to see Dr. Virk's name there with a question mark in Katherine's death. What is his involvement, if any? Is he a witness, a co-conspirator, or a murderer? What's his motivation? Frustration rises in me since he still hasn't been located and held accountable for his role in France. Mario is listed in both investigations with the greatest number of motives with financial gains, a love triangle, a question of blackmail and a connection to both victims. Harriet is also connected to both victims, but a clear motive for Anna is unknown.

Karen points to the board. "The victims are both known to everyone up there, but there seems to be little motive for both murders from these people. Right now, Mario's looking like he has the best motives, but he would have needed an accomplice for Anna's murder. Do we think it was Katherine? I mean, if Mario was willing to have his mother killed, he wouldn't hesitate to kill another person."

"You read my mind," I reply. "Poison was used to kill both people. Poison dart frog venom is exotic; cyanide is more common. Same type of murder weapon, same person, is that what you're thinking?" I look at Caputo.

He throws up his hands. "I am not sure . . . yet."

"I may have told you this already," I say, "but Dr. Virk used inhaled cyanide to kill while we were in France."

Caputo shakes his head. "I've looked through the victim's cell phone records. Katherine has an unidentified number in her phone that may belong to Dr. Virk. If it is his phone, it was a disposable one and hasn't been used or turned on since her death. I have no way of tracking him."

Venom seeps into my voice. "I'm sure he has several burner phones. Toss one and use a new one."

"Katherine's phone shows she called Mario a lot, including on the day of Anna's death. She previously stated she was trying to reach him regarding the situation. Surprisingly, Harriet's phone shows no calls to Mario, at least not the phone at the inn or her personal cell."

Karen leans forward in her chair. "If they each had another phone they used to only call each other, it would help keep the affair secret."

"A search at the inn has not found such a phone." Caputo leans back. "The next time you have dinner at Mi Famiglia, you can share that Katherine was poisoned, but the *polizia* are searching for how. No suspects have been named, but it is still an active investigation."

I stand and extend my hand. "Karen and I have plans for dinner there tonight. I'll let you know if I learn anything new." We shake hands, then Karen and I make our way out of the station.

We walk to the bed-and-breakfast. The streets are more crowded than before. Karen pauses at times to enjoy the costumes and music. When we finally enter the front hall of the inn, we're nearly knocked over by Dani, the pharmacist.

She stops suddenly and looks up with a start. "*Scusa mi,*" she states hastily.

"Hello again," Karen says. "Are you here delivering medication?"

Her reply is clipped. "*Sì, sì.* I must go." She pushes past me in the doorway.

Arthur ambles over to us as Dani disappears into the

crowds. "Nice girl. Came here to pay her respects to Harriet and me because she was friends with Katherine."

Karen knits her brow and stutters an answer. "Ahh, that . . . that was nice of her."

"Yes. Well, must get on, I say," he says as he moves into the library.

Arthur's statement and Dani being here must be something other than what we're told. Back in our room, with the faucets turned on in the bathroom, Karen turns to me. "What the heck is going on in this house? Dani said she was here to deliver medication. Arthur said she was here to pay her respects."

"My coppy senses are going off. There's something there, but what?"

Karen rubs her temples.

"What are you thinking?" I ask.

"Remember how you talked about everyone here being part of a Venn diagram? It's true. I get the feeling that Arthur, Dani, Katherine, Mario, and Harriet have secrets that intersect with other secrets, but no one knows the other's secret."

"Do you mean that they're involved in relationships with each other, or something?"

"Yes and no." She purses her lips as she searches for the right words. "Not relationships like intimate, or at least not all of them, but maybe a side business. Dani's a pharmacist. Is she doing something with drugs that would involve Katherine and/or Arthur? Or Katherine found out and she needed to be silenced? Do you know what I mean?"

I shake my head. "Not fully, no."

"Well, like with the burglaries. We heard those people in

the pharmacy talking. Maybe Dani gives the information to Arthur or someone else."

I look at Karen incredulously. "I don't exactly see Arthur as a stealth cat burglar. Could be anyone associated with the tour company or another person on the tour."

Karen nods. "I agree. I don't know, it could be gun running or human trafficking. But there's something there."

"I fully agree with that. Tonight could be illuminating if we ask the right questions."

"Speaking of questions tonight, what are we trying to find out?" Karen asks.

I rub my forehead. "I'd like more background on both victims and the suspects, too."

"What's our approach? Can I play bad cop?" She lights up and leans into me, wiggling her eyebrows.

I release a deep gut laugh. "I don't think you have bad cop instincts. You do better being kind."

Karen turns her nose up and pretends to pout. "Fine, but I could do bad cop."

"Sure, I believe it," I say without conviction. "Let's take a nap before dinner tonight. I'm tired."

I snuggle into Karen, drift off to sleep, and start a dream. In my dream, Karen and I are on a mattress in the water. The sway of the current rocks me. A bright sun, painted into a clear blue sky, warms me. Tension releases from my body. I'm happy and at peace until clouds start to form. They turn dark, angry, and gray, threatening my calm. The water turns turbulent, the severe waves pushing the mattress from side to side. at risk of turning us over. I wake to find the room dark. Karen's still asleep. I focus on the ceiling until my eyes adjust to the limited light and my breathing slows.

I shake off the foreboding feeling and make my way to the bathroom. A quick shower revives me. I step out, grab a towel, and begin drying off. The light in the bedroom turns on, and Karen screams. I bolt toward her with a towel wrapped around me.

"What?!" I ask.

Karen's eyes are wide with fear. She points to the top of the dresser. There sits a plague doctor mask and an envelope.

CHAPTER 13

"That was not here when we laid down," Karen says shakily.

I grab the envelope and rip it open. Water drips from my hair onto the note.

"Who's it from?" Karen asks. "Please tell me Harriet just dropped off another invitation . . . please?"

I shake my head. "It's from Dr. Virk. He warns us to stop investigating him. He denies having anything to do with either murder and adds that we're lucky to avoid an assault from him the night we were lost in the fog."

Karen frantically looks around the room. "How'd he get in? Do you think he stole keys from Katherine or something? If he did, then he can get in here whenever he likes. Dan, I'm afraid."

I sit on the bed and hug her tight. "I think it's just a warning. If he wanted to hurt us, he could've easily done it."

"What are we going to do? Should we tell Harriet about this?"

I drop to sit on the bed, rubbing my temples. "I don't think we should involve Harriet or Arthur. I don't know what I'll do, but I'll think of something to keep us safe. I'll let Caputo know, too."

My mind is racing with ideas. I'm more committed now to learning Virk's current identity and having him captured.

After dressing, I give Caputo a call. He lets me know he'll be right over. While we wait, a thought occurs to me: if Dr. Virk has keys to our room, he might have keys to the other rooms, like John and Linda's. Is Dr. Virk the thief, or was Katherine?

Karen changes clothes and does her hair and makeup for this evening. I know she's still concerned. She's distracted as she gets ready and keeps mumbling to herself.

I go about rigging up ties to secure the patio doors and mull over what to do to secure our bedroom door when she presents herself. "I'm ready."

"Are you sure you still want to go tonight?" I ask, searching her eyes for confirmation.

She drops her shoulders as she releases a sigh. "Yes. I thought about staying here, but what good would it do? I doubt Virk is coming back tonight. He gave us his warning. Now he'll wait and see what we do."

"Just so you know, I brought my survival switchblade with me, and I plan to carry it. I want us to be safe."

A knock on the door catches my attention. Cautiously, I ask who it is and open the door to find Caputo.

"I came right over. Where is the note?" he asks.

I hold the note out in front of me. He opens an evidence bag, and I drop the note inside.

He looks between Karen and me. "I'll process it for prints. If there are any, hopefully we'll have the name he entered Italy with."

I chuckle. "Good luck with that. Considering Virk hasn't

been captured yet, I doubt he'll leave prints on the note, but you'll find mine."

Caputo nods. "You can come to the station tomorrow to give formal statements." He excuses himself, evidence bag in hand.

Karen hugs me. "Okay, let's go to dinner and try to enjoy it."

I feel my pockets for my wallet, glasses, and knife. Check to all three. We head out of our bedroom and reach the top of the stairs, both of us pausing when we see Arthur in the hall below. I watch, as does Karen. He's opening envelopes and shaking out cards. Money falls from one. He pockets the money as the library door opens and Harriet appears.

"My dear, friends sent along cards of condolences," he tells her.

She stamps her foot. "Leave them on the table. I'll handle any cards or flowers."

"Uh . . . as you wish." He turns and ambles toward the library, failing to mention the money from the card. Curiouser and curiouser. I clear my throat as Karen and I start down the stairs. Harriet looks up and acknowledges us with a slight nod.

"Good evening," Karen and I say in unison as we pass her. I pull open the front door. Cool, salty air enters my nose, and laughter and music make their way to us. I tuck my arm through Karen's. and feel tension. We're both on guard. I scan the crowd before entering the swell of human bodies. My anxiety high, I swivel my head from the front to the sides and spin to look behind me.

The short walk to Mi Famiglia is emotionally exhausting. As we step into the restaurant, I take a couple of deep, cleansing breaths. Karen knows the routine and looks for a chair where my back's to the wall, facing the door, with a sight line to much of the room.

Paul, Lorenzo, and Aldo are seated with drinks in front of them.

"*Bueno sera*," Karen and I say together.

The men raise their glasses to us. I order a round of limoncello for Karen and me as we take our seats.

All of them lean toward me, eyebrows raised. Lorenzo takes the lead. "I saw you enter Caputo's office earlier today. So, what did he tell you about the death?"

I repress a smile. "He confirmed that Katherine's cause of death was poison, but he's waiting for the toxicology report to confirm the type and how it was delivered. He wouldn't name a suspect."

"It was Mario. I am sure of it." Lorenzo leans back in his chair.

Paul shakes his head. "No, I do not trust Harriet. He first husband dies suddenly, and a cause was never discovered. That is what I heard."

"No, that is not the truth. Her first husband had a heart attack. Nothing suspicious," remarks Lorenzo with a dismissive wave of his hand.

"The murderer could be Arthur," Aldo says. "I heard that when he was in the army, he competed for a colonel position with his best friend. The friend had a training accident one night and died. Arthur was not blamed for anything, and he got the promotion. I do not trust him."

Paul waves his finger at him. "Harriet got her husband's money. She wants Arthur's money, too."

"Arthur has money?" Karen asks with her brow creased.

"*Sì, sì,*" Paul replies. "His family is very wealthy, from York in England. Big house, land, and stable. His brother owns it now, but when he dies, then Arthur gets it."

"But how would Harriet inherit? Aren't there other family members?" I ask.

"All dead. The brother has cancer and will die soon. He has no wife and no children. Arthur is the last," Paul says matter-of-factly.

I run scenarios in my head. If Harriet wants the money but not Arthur, she'll need to wait for his brother to pass so he can inherit. It would still take time to transfer everything before she could remove Arthur from her life. So why did Katherine die? She's not in line to inherit from her stepfather. I ask the group these questions.

Enzo snaps at me, exasperated. "She knows who the burglar is, and they killed her to keep her quiet." He holds up his finger for emphasis. "Or she killed Anna and Mario took revenge because he loved his mama."

"Pfft" escapes from Paul's mouth. "Katherine was blackmailing someone. She had a lot of money but didn't work. She knew something she should not have and used it."

"You are all wrong," Enzo says, laughing. "Mario just proposed to Dani. She plans to sell the pharmacy and join him as a drug salesman in the same company he works for. They make very good money."

Lorenzo sits upright. "No, Mario said Harriet is in love with him. Katherine was a caregiver to some elderly people, was caught stealing from them, then was fired, which is why she lived with her mother."

The conversation stops as the appetizers arrive: a platter of bruschetta and another of prosciutto with Brie and melon, along with slices of bread.

Plates are filled and passed. I order two bottles of red wine and a round of limoncello.

I look up at Lorenzo. "What about that guy Katherine was dating? I think maybe he's a doctor?" I show them a picture of Dr. Virk on my phone from our time in France.

He nods. "I do not think he is a doctor. They do not like him. They thought he was no good, but Katherine said he is very rich."

"Who do you mean by 'them'?" Karen asks.

"Arthur and Harriet, but when Harriet heard he was rich, she wanted him to buy Casa de Inglese." Aldo releases a hearty laugh.

I rub my chin thoughtfully. "I can't remember his name. Do you know what it is?"

"It's a stupid name," Aldo spits out vehemently, his lips pressed together. "His last name is Vita, which is *italiano* for 'life.' It sounds Italian, but he is not Italian."

Karen asks him, "Do you know his first name?"

He taps his forehead. "Ummm, it is another stupid name. Uhhh, Skanda. Yes, that is it. Skanda Vita. He is staying at the Casa Riviera del Felice. I have family staying there, and I saw him there."

I want to jump up and cheer, "I've got you, Dr. Virk!", repressing the urge to call Caputo and report this information immediately. My enthusiasm is curbed because dinner arrives: spaghetti with fresh tomato sauce and basil, shrimp scampi,

and ravioli with spinach and gorgonzola, topped with wal-
nuts. I'm almost too excited to sit still and eat, my mind full
of thoughts of Virk, or rather Vita, making his escape as he
learns I know his new name. Karen makes eye contact with
me and gives me a half smile. She appreciates my excitement,
but more importantly that we are here now. I sit and try to enjoy this moment with good food, great company, and the best
news of all, Dr. Virk's name and location.

As the first bite of spaghetti touches my tongue, I look
around and realize I'm privileged to be here with Karen and
these men. I take a deep breath and slow my breathing down
to enjoy this food and friends.

CHAPTER 14

Now that I know more about Virk, I feel much better being in Venice with him. I'm on the offense.

"Is it too late to call Caputo with what we know about Virk?" I ask Karen as we walk home.

She shakes her head. "Dan, it's 11:30 at night. I think the poor man might just be asleep."

"Fine, but I'm anxious to see Virk captured. I don't think I'll sleep until he's in custody."

Once in our room, Karen and I crawl into bed. My mind runs possible scenarios of capturing Virk. Will he fight, or will he surrender? Or a little of both? After tossing and turning for a while, I fall asleep.

Karen sits up and screams my name.

I push up on my elbows, looking around the room while trying to comprehend where I am. "What's wrong?" I ask.

Her breathing is rapid and shallow. "I'm sorry. I had another dream. I was chasing Virk, and we were running up and down staircases until we reached the Bridge of Sighs. You were there and grabbed Virk's arm to arrest him. You were shouting, 'I've got you, Virk! I got you!', but when he turned around, he looked like Virk, but it wasn't him. You had your knife, and he was trying to grab it. So I screamed for you to be careful."

I flop back against my pillow. A feeling of dread comes over me. What if, even with the new information, Virk isn't caught? Will that escalate his vendetta against us? Karen puts her arm across my chest and cuddles into me.

When the sun is up, so are we. After we finish breakfast, we head to the station to give Caputo our statement about Virk's note in our room.

"Anything on the note?" I ask.

He shakes his head. "No, just your fingerprints. Nothing special about the paper it was written on."

He asks what information I learned the night before, sitting up straighter when we tell of Casa Riviera del Felice. He leans forward with his elbows on his desk, his fingertips pressed together, appearing to mull over everything. Finally, he stands up and motions for us to follow him. He leads us down to where the police patrol boats are kept.

"Get in," Caputo says. "We will go to Casa Riviera del Felice. This is quicker than walking through the crowds." He sits next to the driver while Karen and I maneuver to the back seats.

The officer driving maneuvers the boat backwards with ease. My heart jumps a little at experiencing this. Karen smiles at me. She's enjoying the ride too.

Caputo leans back and shouts at us, "Antonio is one of the best drivers we have. He is a fifth-generation boat driver on these waters and second-generation police officer. He knows where every log or other hazard is."

The boat skims across the water quickly and effortlessly

for the short ride along the Grand Canal. In a small alleyway, we pass under laundry hanging from lines strung between houses. Antonio positions us next to a dilapidated pier, and we get off. A flight of steep, cracked, and, in some places, missing concrete stairs lead up to the street. Before us stands a white stucco, two-story building.

Caputo points to the building. "This is Casa Riviera del Felice."

I take a couple of deep breaths to resist the temptation to run up to the door. Caputo climbs the stairs with catlike ease, taking the lead as we knock on the front door. A woman opens the door, her dark hair pulled to a tight bun at the nape of her neck as she wipes her hands on an apron. Caputo speaks with her in Italian and shows his badge. She points to a room down the corridor straight in front of us. Thanking her, he steps inside. She moves to the end of the hall while Karen and I enter the home.

"She says that a man with the name Skanda Vita is registered here and is still in his room. Wait here while I check," Caputo orders.

I position myself with a view of the hall and watch as Caputo walks in that direction. He stops a few doors down and knocks. The door opens, but the person remains out of sight. I strain to hear what is being said, but both Caputo's and Virk's voices are too quiet. I pace back and forth, squeezing and releasing my fists as I wait. Finally, Caputo waves me over. My heart leaps, and I hold my breath as I quickly stride to face Dr. Virk. I round the doorframe to come before him.

One look and my hopes crash, this man is similar in build and looks but it isn't Virk. "No," I spit out.

Karen's dream was right. We thought we had him, but we never really did. I know Virk arranged this situation to confuse the police and undermine my search for him.

I walk back to Karen and let her know what we found. She takes my hand and holds it tight.

Caputo comes to my side. "I spoke to him. This man has identification of who he is. He entered the country legally and was offered this paid reservation several days ago, took it, and didn't ask many questions of the person offering him the room. The inn's owner was not told any of this. He confirmed the person who approached him looked Middle Eastern but didn't give his name." He sighs. "I am sorry. This is not the result you were hoping for."

I shake my head. "It was too easy. I should've known Virk would never be that stupid once he knew that I knew he was in Venice."

We make our way back down to the police boat. The ride back to the station is quiet and feels much longer.

Once off the boat, Karen and I make our way back to our bed-and-breakfast. In our room, Karen looks at me. "Virk seems to be playing the long game and doing it boldly," she says. "That took some backbone to come into our room while we were here. I think, for now, we should stop actively pursuing him. We'll get him eventually."

I know she's right. It's just wrong that he's enjoying himself. He needs to answer for his participation in the situation in France.

"You're right," I say with no enthusiasm. My phone chimes with a text message. "Paul is on his way."

Karen's hands fly up to her mouth. "I totally forgot. We made arrangements for a tour of Murano today. I'm ready to go, if you are."

I muster as much joy as I can. "Yeah. It'll be fun."

Karen and I meet Paul in the lobby. He's dressed in a soft blue knit shirt and khaki shorts with blue boat shoes.

"Come, I have a boat waiting," Paul states quietly, waving us toward the door. At the dock is Marco, the boat driver who picked us up at the airport. I shake his hand. "Good to see you again."

"*Sì, sì.* Hope you have been enjoying Carnival," he replies.

I'm at a loss for words to adequately describe our vacation to this point, so I just nod.

Once we're seated, Marco backs the boat away from the dock and points it in the direction of a piece of land in the distance.

Karen takes my hand. She's beaming with joy as the boat glides over the water. I force myself to push the disappointment of not having Virk in custody from my mind. Karen wants to enjoy this day, and I want it for her. I recline into the leather seats with the breeze and an occasional water spritz in my face. The sun is out. Upbeat music reaches us from the shore. The smell of saltwater enters my nose. I breathe deeply and slowly. Venice recessed behind us. The waterway expands with more traffic and diversity in boat styles. Upon approaching the island, small fishing cottages become visible in soft, muted hues of blues, greens, yellows, and more. Marco slows the boat and effortlessly maneuvers it to the dock.

Paul, Karen, and I step onto the dock. Paul says something

to Marco in Italian, which I hope is a time to return to pick us up. I chuckle to myself.

Paul moves us toward the line to enter the glassblowing factory. He speaks to the person checking people in, and we are allowed to enter. Inside, we find a square room painted battleship-gray with a small stage in front followed by black wrought iron bleachers. We find seats to view the demonstration.

The room fills with approximately thirty people. "This is in English," Paul assures us.

A middle-aged man with gray-tinged hair steps onto the stage. "Good day to you all. My name is Luca. I will give you a brief history of glassblowing on Murano, then a master glassblower will demonstrate how it's done."

I find myself leaning forward in my seat as he speaks. I have a hard time hearing in a crowd, but I'm also anticipating the show.

Luca continues, "The history of glassmaking in Murano dates back to 1291 when the Venetian government ordered the glassmakers of Venice to relocate as a precaution against fires. This small island emerged as one of the most prominent centers for glassmaking in the world. Today you will see firsthand the artists handcrafting glass. Using silica, soda, lime, and potassium, glassmakers melt the elements together at a temperature of fifteen hundred degrees Celsius."

Luca holds up several colors of the same vase. "Different minerals can be added to make the vibrant colors. Zinc is added for white, cobalt for blue, and others. The liquid glass mixture is mouth-blown and handcrafted by master glassblowers in a series of elaborate steps. Now we go to the shop."

The crowd follows Luca to the workshop. A staff member

pulls a long tube from an oven and begins to blow into it, forming a bubble at the other end. The tube is twirled, blown, then returned to the fire, and the process is repeated. The staff member removes the glass piece from the end with large pliers and places it on a ceramic board. "You can have this for free if you can hold it." He then places a piece of paper on the glass, which ignites into flames. "Ohhhhh" is collectively stated by the crowd.

Karen whispers to me that the thought crossed her mind to try and touch it. I look at her with wide eyes.

"But I didn't," she quips.

Luca announces that the tour is over, but we are welcome to browse the gift shop.

Karen stands in the middle of the showroom. "I could spend a million dollars here. Everything is just so beautiful." She spots the Christmas ornaments, choosing a deep blue-and-gold crackled color in the shape of a bunch of grapes. I head to the counter to pay for it. Once the ornament is paid for and wrapped, I find Karen outside in the courtyard.

I hand her the package. "I need to find a restroom before heading back."

"I'll be here," she replies.

It takes me a few minutes to find the bathroom. When I'm done, I return to the courtyard and see Karen speaking to an elderly woman dressed head to toe in black lace, including over her face. The woman moves along the sidewalk and disappears around the corner.

"Who was that?" I ask Karen.

"I don't know. She offered to do a tarot card reading, so I thought, why not?" Karen shrugs. "It was fun. She had me pick three cards. One each for my past, present, and future. First was The High Priestess, then The Lovers and finally The Moon. Can you guess what she said were their meanings?"

I place my finger to my lips and try to think of their symbolism. "I'd say you and I are The Lovers. The High Priestess, I think wise and insightful, so that would be you."

Karen nods. I continue, "I'm lost on what the last one means."

She laughs. "The Moon card faced down, not up. It can mean inner confusion, darkness, insecurity, and misinterpretations of what something seems to be. I'm not quite sure about that one."

"Feels like these murders." I chuckle. "Still sounds cool."

Karen smiles. "It was. I've never had a tarot reading before. I offered the woman a few euros, and her hand was ice-cold when I placed the money in it. She must have very little circulation in her fingers."

Paul joins us, and we follow him to the boat landing. The ride back has me a bit happier since the disappointment this morning. Once we arrive at the pier near the inn, I shake Marco's hand and pass a few euros to him. He makes eye contact with me. I wink. He nods acknowledgement.

Karen and I thank Paul for a wonderful time. He waves goodbye to us and heads into the throng of people. Karen links her arm through mine. "I'm not hungry now, but maybe later we can head to Il Sogno."

"Sounds like a plan," I reply and pull her closer to me.

CHAPTER 15

Karen and I meander our way to the restaurant, which is unusually quiet. The sun is fading, and dusk is settling in the city.

Andrea greets us. "I have my best table for you. Come with me." He leads us to a table with a view of the canal. Lights in the area are coming on, and the city appears to sparkle. It *is* really a beautiful and romantic city. After scanning the menus and giving Andrea our orders of drinks and appetizers, Karen and I sit back and watch the canal.

Andrea is back with a sangria for Karen and a beer for me. We sip our drinks, watching the variety of boats. All makes, models, sizes, and dollar amounts pass by. I wonder if it's ever quiet.

"If the boats could talk, I wonder what stories they would tell," Karen remarks, pointing to a white speedboat with aqua stripes as it races through the water. "I think he feels the need to go that fast because his mother never hugged him and the family dog prefers his sister."

"I'd say that his wife is out of town and he can't wait to see his girlfriend."

Karen laughs out loud. "That's naughty, but funny." She points to an elderly couple in a gleaming wooden boat. "What about them?"

"They've been in love from the first time they met over fifty years ago, and still are."

"Ahhh, that's so romantic," Karen says, squeezing my hand.

Amata is clearing a nearby table, and Karen waves to her. She presses a grin to her lips.

Andrea returns and places our choices on the table. Mussels and clams in white sauce, bruschetta with tomatoes and garlic, prosciutto, melons, and cheese, along with slices of bread.

"Oh, that looks wonderful. Thank you," Karen says.

Andrea bows slightly before heading back to the kitchen. We each make up a plate. Every bite is flavorful and satisfying. We clink glasses and toast to the evening, the food, and being happy together. Andrea checks back once we are nearly done.

Karen smiles at him. "It is all delicious."

"Would you be able to sit and have a drink with us?" I ask.

Andrea's mouselike face twitches from side to side before he smiles and sits down. "Amata!" he calls out. She comes to the table. "Bring my favorite wine and three glasses."

She knits her brow together and looks between us. Andrea nods to her. She turns and walks back into the restaurant.

"I will share my favorite wine. It is just for special times. You like red wine, yes?" he asks.

I open my mouth and close it again, as I don't but want to be kind at his gesture.

Amata returns with a bottle of wine, three glasses, and a bottle opener. After cutting the seal around the neck of the bottle and pushing in the corkscrew, Andrea pulls the cork from the bottle with a dramatic fling of his arm. Karen and I clap. He fills all of the glasses and hands one to each of us.

We raise them. "How would you say 'cheers' in Italian?" Karen asks Andrea.

He replies, "*Cin-cin.*" We clink glasses and say "*cin-cin*" in unison.

Karen tastes hers as she's not a wine drinker. I take a small sip. Andrea gulps his and refills his glass half-full. He brings the glass to his nose and inhales. "When I smell this wine, and when I taste it, I smile because it is my memories of my grandmother's kitchen. I was a boy there. It smells earthy, with a hint of clover and lavender." . He finishes his second glass, placing it on the table with a thud. He closes his eyes, leans back in his chair, and releases a long, deep sigh.

"Do you feel all right?" Karen asks, touching his arm.

"*Sì*. Carnival is a busy time," he says.

Karen raises her glass to him. "I'm honored that you shared this with us."

Andrea stands, then bows slightly. "Please take the bottle to finish." He looks to the restaurant entrance. Teresa is in the doorway, glaring in our direction. "I must go," Andrea says, and hurries to the kitchen.

I rest my elbows on the table. "I don't know about you, but I'm not a fan of this wine. It's too dry and has an aftertaste I can't describe. I don't want to hurt Andrea's feelings."

"Well, I'm no expert, but I don't care for it either," Karen replies. She discreetly pours her unfinished glass into the canal. We switch glasses, and she repeats the action.

Karen leans toward me. "I don't know about his taste in wine, but the food here is awesome."

She finishes the bruschetta, and I soak the last piece of

bread in the wine sauce. With a smack of my lips, I lean back in my chair.

Karen holds her sangria, her other hand in mine. The sun has disappeared as we sit under the string lights overhead.

"This was great. I'm glad we're here," she states, squeezing my hand.

Life on the canal continues. We sit and watch this disorganized dance of boats making their way through the water.

As Amata begins to clear away our plates, our tranquility is shattered by a crash and screaming coming from inside the restaurant. We both are on our feet. I run—well, not so much a run as a fast lope to the entrance. I find Teresa standing in the small dining room. Andrea is lying on his side on the floor between two tables, vomit covering his shirt. I rush to him, feel for a pulse, and find none. Teresa speaks rapidly in Italian to me. I can't catch a word I understand. Karen comes by my side.

"Call Caputo," I snap at her. She nods and dials her phone.

I stand up to face Teresa. "What happened?" I demand more authoritatively than I meant to.

Wide-eyed, she looks at me. "He said that his heart was racing, and he felt sick, then he fell into the table and the floor."

Karen breaks in, "Caputo is on his way. He said not to touch anything."

I roll my eyes. Amata stands in the doorway of the restaurant.

I look between her and Teresa. "Did he say anything about feeling sick before this?" Both shake their heads. "Did he drink or eat anything here or at home?" I continue.

Again, they shake their heads.

"Dan, he had wine with us." Karen points in the direction of our table.

My head snaps up and I'm on my feet, racing toward the table. Once there, I halt. The table is clear. No wine bottle, glasses, or plates. "Did you take the things off?" I accuse Amata, who's standing behind me.

"No, no, I touched nothing," she quietly replies, stepping back from me.

I rub my hands over my face. "Great!" I snap sarcastically. "If there was evidence in the bottle or the glass, they're gone now." I walk back to the entrance of the restaurant to stand guard over the scene until the police arrive.

"Dan, if something dangerous was in the wine, I'm worried about you," Karen whispers in my ear. "You drank more than I did. Do you feel sick?"

I pat her arm and give her a quick wink. "No, I'm fine."

She sets her lips in a hard line. I doubt she believes me. I'm not sure I believe me

Caputo arrives with a team of officers behind him. "What happened here? Has anything been touched or moved?" He glares in my direction, then Karen's. "You two *again* near a death."

"Sorry," I reply. I believe there's a good chance that Karen and I are not coming off the suspect board.

He dismissively waves his hand at us. "Wait outside for me. I will talk with Teresa and Amata."

While he gives orders to the other members of his team, a crowd begins to form near the doorway. One of the officers guards the entrance. Karen and I move past him to the outside and sit at an empty table.

"At the rate we're finding dead bodies, the police may make us stay as people of interest." Karen laughs.

"Or some of the usual suspects," I add.

I look out over the water. Nothing has changed. Boats of locals and tourists carrying out their day. Life in Venice goes on. Time passes slowly, which is juxtaposed to the scene out on the canal. Tradition versus current trends.

Lorenzo notices us with surprise on his face and walks straight to our table. "You were here when the death occurred?"

"Yes," I reply.

He pulls out his phone, taps an app, and places it near me on the table. "This is a sad. I want to report this as the tragic day it is. Tell me what you know."

"Umm . . . not much," I say hesitantly. I'm in an awkward position here between finding out what Caputo knows and what Lorenzo knows. I'd hoped to speak to both of them informally, to learn something that will help solve these murders. I tap Lorenzo's phone. "I'm waiting to talk to Caputo. Maybe we can meet later tonight . . . say, seven o'clock at Mi Famiglia?"

Simultaneously, we notice Caputo heading toward us. Lorenzo bumps my hand and nods.

Once Caputo arrives at our table, he asks Karen and Lorenzo to step away. I get it. Always interview witnesses and/or suspects separately. Karen moves to a table closer to the restaurant. Lorenzo goes to speak with Teresa.

"What did you tell Lorenzo?" Caputo asks, his voice stern and cold.

"Nothing," I snap back. "I know to speak with the investigator first."

He drops into a chair, rubbing his eyes. His face is the ashen hue of fatigue. "What can you tell me about what happened?"

I summarize what I experienced, including the missing bottle and glasses.

"Did you touch anything?" he asks.

"No."

"Did you move the body at all?"

"No. I felt for a pulse and didn't find one. CPR wouldn't have helped. He was dead."

Caputo leans back with his eyes closed. Either he's hoping this is all a bad dream or he actually fell asleep. I sit quietly, waiting to see what he does next. Moments later, he releases a long, deep sigh, opens his eyes, and sits up straight. "Okay, describe what happened one more time. Do not leave anything out."

I open my mouth to start talking when he holds up one finger, pulls a notebook and pen from his back pocket, flips open the notebook, and looks directly at me. Again, I explain everything I know that happened. Caputo makes notes. When I finish the second time, he snaps the book closed. "I will need you to come to my office and make an official report, *again*."

I nod. "We can be there this afternoon, if that works for you?"

The reply is short and curt. "Fine."

I sit and look out over the water, playing and replaying the last moments of Andrea's life with us as Caputo leaves to question Karen. When their interview is over, Karen joins me at the table.

"I don't think Caputo is happy with us," she states with a grimace. I agree with that thought.

The *commissario* returns to our table. "I plan to interview Teresa and Amata again while the tech guys work. You can go, but do not forget to come to my office, *si?*"

"Yes, we'll be there," I assure him.

Caputo heads for the restaurant while Karen and I go back to our bed-and-breakfast. "I wish there was something we could do to help." I replay the scene in my mind. Did I miss something? Who are the best suspects?

Karen furrows her brow and tilts her head. "We've got supplies back in our room to work on our own suspect board."

Her statement causes me to abruptly stop walking. Karen bumps into my arm.

"What's wrong?" she asks.

"You talking about investigating and doing more on the suspect board . . . are you sure?"

Karen sucks in a deep breath. "Dan, this just keeps getting worse. Three murders of people we knew. If we can help Caputo, then let's do it to try and get an answer," she snaps, then strides off toward the inn.

I hurry my pace to catch up with her. Secretly, I'm energized by the thought of an investigation, but I know better than to say that where Karen can hear it. I liked Andrea, and the thought of someone getting away with his murder just pisses me off. I want the person or persons involved with all of these murders to be stopped.

CHAPTER 16

Back in our room, Karen pulls out paper and her Venetian mask pen. "I'll write down the name of each victim and lay them down in separate columns on the dresser. You give me names of suspects and their connection to the victim, with a possible motive."

I nod. "First is Mario. He's connected to Anna, his mother, and wanted her to sell her shop, but she refused. Would he kill his own mother? He'd have killed Katherine for revenge if she'd caused Anna's death because she wanted more and Anna didn't approve of their relationship. Why kill Andrea?"

Karen cocks her head. "Arthur didn't like his stepdaughter, but is that enough to kill her? I can't think of a reason for him to harm either Anna or Andrea. I doubt Harriet would kill her daughter, and she did have Teresa and Andrea cater her ball."

I drum my fingers on the dresser until Karen puts her hand on mine to make it stop.

Karen chews on the end of her pen, then points it to the paper. "I can't see any reason for Arielle to want any of them dead. Dani possibly wants to be with Mario, so Anna may have been a problem, but it looked as if she and Katherine were friends."

"That brings us to Teresa," I say. "Did she want a divorce

from Andrea or control of the restaurant? Life insurance is a good motive, especially if it appears to be natural causes. However, there's no direct motive for Anna or Katherine, unless Teresa's interested in Mario, then both women could be in her way." I sit on the bed with my head in my hands.

Karen rubs my back. I don't see a pattern that connects all the victims to one suspect. Do we have three murderers that all decided this week was a good time to kill their victims? That seems unlikely.

"What's the thread that links all the victims together?" I say. "We can't rule out Dr. Virk, Vita, whatever."

Karen presses her fingertips together, her eyes looking over each item. "I don't think he had a reason for Anna or Andrea. Katherine, maybe, but he had already made sure he wouldn't be found at the bed-and-breakfast."

She's right. We sit quietly, but not a single person comes to the top of the list. I lay back on the bed and close my eyes.

Karen shakes me. "What?" I ask with an edge in my voice.

"We need to get to Caputo's office to give our statements." She laughs. "Take our credit card, if we need to post bail."

I shake my head. "Normally there's no bail for murder."

She crosses her arms over her chest. "I hear the Bridge of Sighs calling our names."

We head outside, weaving and dodging the revelers throughout the square. I sense less joy in the air, or it could just be me. I'm saddened at the thought of Andrea's death.

At the police station, the officer at the door contacts Caputo, who escorts us to his office. His eyes are sunken and red. I don't think he's sleeping at this point.

Karen and I are placed in separate rooms. Caputo enters my room and asks that I repeat my observations of Andrea's death while he takes it down on paper. When I'm finished, he hands me the paper, then has me read it and sign at the bottom. I follow him to his office, and Karen joins us there. A uniformed officer hands him papers that I assume is Karen's statement. He gives the officer a curt nod before the officer leaves, closing the door behind him. Caputo places the papers on his desk and looks directly at me. "Well?"

"Well . . . what?" I ask.

"Ideas, thoughts, leads, plans to leave Italy soon?" He leans back in his chair, his fingertips pressed together.

"No to all of the above," I quickly reply, then add, "Do you believe that Karen and I had anything to do with these murders?"

He sucks in a deep breath. "No, but whatever you are doing to be present when a murder occurs, please stop. There is a great deal of pressure to solve these crimes, including the thefts."

"We"—I wave my thumb between me and Karen—"have plans to meet with Lorenzo and hopefully others to exchange information. I'll let you know if I learn anything." I cross my arms over my chest. "Change of subject, any update on locating Dr. Virk?"

Caputo shakes his head. "I've been reviewing airport security video when I have time, but without an exact date that he entered, I don't know how far back I need to look."

"Or he could have left, now that he knows we're looking for him," I growl, squeezing my fists together.

Caputo stands up behind his desk. Karen and I take it as our cue to leave.

Outside, Karen grabs my hand. "Can we do something different this afternoon? No investigating? Let's explore this city . . . you know, shop and maybe find a new bar. We haven't been to Harry's Bar yet for a bellini."

We hook arms and stride forward with emphasis and no idea where we're going, but this is an "aventure," as our son used to say.

We meander through alleyways and over bridges until Karen finds a store with inexpensive Venetian masks. She buys one for each grandchild. Once they're securely wrapped in a paper bag, I'm entrusted to carry the treasures until my knees let me know they need a rest.

We make our way to Harry's Bar, set along the Grand Canal. It's a white stone building, with two oversized brown wooden doors and amber glass windows with petite, decorative, black wrought iron bars. We step inside to the 1930s: brown wooden bar, barstools, and booths. I survey the room in case Ernest Hemingway, Gertrude Stein, or another of their contemporaries is seated in a distant corner. Disappointed, I don't find any. A young couple occupying a table to the far left are the only other patrons.

A waiter in a classic suit of black pants, a waistcoat, and a crisp white shirt greets us. I ask for a booth for two. He has us follow him to the far corner with a full view of the bar, handing us menus when we're seated. We peruse them.

"I know I'm having a bellini. The legend is the drink was invented here," Karen remarks.

"What's in a bellini?" I ask.

Karen grins at me. "Peach puree and prosecco. Yum."

"What the heck, I'll get one too."

The drinks arrive in chilled fluted glasses.

"I'd say *'cin-cin'* except it makes me sad to think of Andrea, so cheers," Karen says quietly.

"Cheers." We tap glasses. The drink is slightly sweet, bubbly, and refreshing. Karen hums softly after her first sip. After finishing our wonderful light lunch of ham sandwiches with melon, we decide on another round of bellinis. We sit back and enjoy people-watching as the place fills up with costumed customers.

Once we're done, we make our way back to the inn, enjoying the festive energy of the musicians and revelers on the streets. We open the front door to hear Arthur's voice hissing from the library. I make my way closer.

"This will never do," he says.

A mumbled response follows. I can't make out the words or who the voice belongs to.

Arthur answers, "We haven't come this far to stop. I need a fresh start."

I inch closer, hoping to identify the other person, but I don't have a direct sight line and the other person doesn't enunciate. I decide to open the door to the library, pretending I did it accidentally . . . well, more on purpose, when Paul Aiello enters the hall from the kitchen. "Ahh, Dan, Karen, you are here."

My entire body cringes and I let go of the doorknob.

He continues, "I would like to arrange a walking architectural tour of the city."

Arthur closes the library door with a distinctive bang. So much for learning more of what was being discussed and with whom.

Karen steps next to me. "Paul, that's very kind of you. Dan and I will think about it and let you know."

"*Sì, sì*. Very good." He waves good-bye and heads out the front door.

Karen winks at me. "I'd like to sit down here and read awhile."

"That's a great idea," I reply, pointing my head in the direction of the library. She nods.

We sit in the hall and begin to read from our phones. Arthur steps from the library, closing the door behind him. "Good to see you again. Hello, my dear."

"Hello," Karen and I reply in unison.

Arthur looks as if he's searching for something or someone when he makes eye contact with me. "Anything I can help you with? Was that Paul fellow just here?"

Karen smiles sweetly at Arthur. "Yes. He kindly offered us a walking tour of Venice."

"Good, good. Well, must be off," he says, then strolls toward the kitchen.

My eyes flick toward the library, then between the kitchen and the library. I'm debating on whether or not to open the door. I review my options: one, just open the library door, or two, wait long enough for someone to emerge. Unfortunately, I wait too long to barge into the library.

Arthur strolls back into the lobby from the kitchen with a ceramic mug in hand. "Tea, old man?" Steam rises from the cup. "Fresh pot in the kitchen, and there's biscuits too."

I shake my head. "No, thank you." Karen also declines tea. He barely opens the door before slipping into the library.

Karen stands up. "Dan, this isn't going to work," she whispers. "He knows we're here. If he's planning something with someone else, he'll wait until we leave. Let's head upstairs."

I put away my phone and stand up. She's right. A stakeout doesn't work once you've been spotted. As we climb the stairs, I can't help but think about Arthur's words. What is he planning, if anything? What did he mean by 'coming this far' and 'needing a fresh start'? Did he cause Katherine's death? Or now that she's dead, is Harriet in danger? Who'd he confide in? A co-conspirator, or was he threatening someone he views as standing in his way?

CHAPTER 17

Once in our room, Karen turns to me. "I don't know about you, but I could use a cup of tea."

That's all the motivation I need to step out of our room, creep my way to the balcony, and slowly make my way down the stairs while watching the library door. I'm so focused on seeing who comes that I fail to realize that there's two stairs left and not one. My foot lands on the floor of the hall with a resounding *thud*, and I let out a "whoa."

I fail the ninja 101 approach. The library door swings open, and Harriet steps into the frame. "Was that you who made that noise?"

Caught off guard by seeing her there, I stutter for a reasonable response. "Aaaahh, ummm, yeah." *Great comeback, Dan.*

She shifts her weight to one side, places her right hand on her hip, and laser-focuses her blue eyes on me. "Well? Is there something you need?"

I croak out, "Tea."

"In the kitchen. Help yourself." She spins on her heels and steps back into the library.

I blow out a sigh. Ace detective, I'm not. I head for the kitchen, pour two cups of tea, add milk and sugar to Karen's, and pocket a couple of biscuits. Traversing slowly through the hall and back up the stairs, I try not to spill.

"Well?" Karen asks impatiently, leaning forward on the bed. "Did you see who it was?"

"Harriet," I say blandly.

She opens her mouth to speak, then closes it. A deep frown appears on her face. "No way."

"That's my thought. Arthur's voice was assertive, or at least self-assured. I've never heard him speak to Harriet that way. Maybe the person who was there left while we were in our room? Curiouser and curiouser."

"Then who do you think he was talking to?"

I rub my forehead. "No clue."

Karen takes a sip of tea. "Oh, that's hot." She blows on her cup.

"Careful, the tea's hot," I snicker out loud.

"Ha, ha," Karen remarks with a dose of sarcasm. She nibbles around the edges of her biscuit. "This is a mess. Anna was killed first, but why?"

"She stood in the way of someone. Katherine? Dani? Harriet? If she was removed for whoever to get what they wanted . . . like Mario or the sale of the shop, then Katherine was killed because she caused Anna's death, or was linked to whoever did the killing. That would explain those murders, but then there's Andrea."

"Let's see if we can talk to Teresa and maybe Amata. We can express our condolences," Karen states,. "Really, we need to ask if there's anything they know, I mean need, at this time."

I nod. "I like the way you think. Let's go to the restaurant to see if it's done being a crime scene."

We step out of our room and bump into John and Linda, their luggage in hand.

Karen looks at them with surprise. "Are you guys leaving? Before the grand ball?"

"Yes. I've had enough of this place," Linda snaps with a hard set to her mouth.

I add, "Have you cleared leaving with the police?"

John nods. "Yes, the police are aware. Good to meet you both, but Linda has her mind made up." He puts his hand out, which I shake. "We're headed for New York!" He nods to me, and I return the gesture, then they turn and head down the stairs. Harriet stops them in the hall before they leave.

Karen and I look at each other, not knowing what to say. We make our way down the stairs and out onto the street. My mind swirls with different approaches as we dodge people along the Grand Canal. I convince Karen to take the lead in trying to tease out motives and suspects.

My shoulders relax once we're there. The police tape is gone, and the door is open.

Karen leans in through the doorway. Amata blocks the entrance before Karen can step inside. "Do you need something, *signora*?"

Karen touches Amata's arm, which she withdraws as if stung. Karen smiles. "Dan and I wanted to come back and tell you and Teresa how sorry we are about Andrea."

"*Sì, sì*, it is very sad," she concedes.

"I'm surprised that the restaurant is open so soon," Karen says in a calm, soothing voice.

Teresa steps out from the kitchen. "This is *my* business

now. We need to clean after the *polizia* made a mess. We will open tomorrow. If we are not open, then we have no money," she snaps, her arms crossed over her chest.

Karen smiles back at her. "Andrea would've never wanted you to suffer financially. It's great to see you carrying on his dream, because that's what Il Sogno means . . . 'the dream,' right?"

"Pfft" escapes Amata's mouth. "His dream, no her dream." She points to Teresa. "She is a great chef, but he would not let her put any of her recipes on the menu," Amata states emphatically.

"I had no idea," Karen says, dropping her shoulders and looking between Teresa and Amata. "Will you stay on and run the restaurant together?"

Teresa draws her lips into a hard line. "Do you want something? We are not open today!"

I look over Teresa's and Amata's shoulders. There aren't any customers, but workmen are piling tables on top of each other. "It looks more like you're closing the restaurant."

Teresa's eyes narrow. "This is my business. *Scusi.*" She reaches for the door, pushing it closed, forcing me and Karen to step back from the doorway.

We walk several blocks before Karen turns to me. "What the heck was that? Her dream, not his, blah, blah, blah."

"Caputo needs to know if Teresa is planning to sell and move out of Venice." I dial my phone and relay what we just learned. He states he'll follow up with Teresa.

"Let's head to Mi Famiglia to meet Lorenzo," I say, nudging Karen's arm.

Rain starts as we make our way there and gladly step into

the warmth. Lorenzo is at a table with Paul. Karen and I join them. I order a round of limoncello.

Lorenzo leans forward, his elbows on the table. "Did Caputo tell you anything about the investigation?"

"Well, luckily he doesn't suspect me or Karen of being hired killers." I laugh.

Paul looks at me. "Why would he think that?"

Lorenzo slaps Paul's back. "He is making a joke."

Paul's face and neck redden in response.

I chime in. "Seriously, he didn't say anything. We were there to give our statements because we were with Andrea right before he died. I didn't see anything strange except Andrea looking tired."

"That wife of his would make anyone tired," Lorenzo spews. "Always yelling, never happy. She told the police that Andrea was abusive to her. Ha." He shakes his head.

"Are you saying that she lied to the police?" Karen asks.

Paul jumps in. "*Sì*, Amata did too. She told the same story, but it is not true. Andrea told me that Teresa wants to sell the restaurant and move to New York, but Andrea was happy in Venice. They had many fights about it. She thinks herself a great chef." He spits on the floor.

"I have told Caputo that they have both lied," Lorenzo states.

When we first met Amata, Paul told us that she was just back from a trip to New York. Was she there to set up a new situation for Teresa and herself? Was there a plan in place to kill Andrea?

Karen interrupts my thoughts. "Oh, Paul, before I forget,

Dan and I would love to do a walking tour. Thank you for stopping by to ask."

A frown crosses his face. "I thought of the tour when I saw you. I was there because Harriet needed the pictures I took of the inn to give to her realtor."

Karen purses her lips. "I'm confused. I heard Harriet tell Arthur that you're doing an article on the inn for a travel magazine and she hopes that it increases business. That's why you took the pictures."

He shakes his head. "She wants to sell and move back to England where her husband has family money."

"I'm sure that place is sad for her with her daughter being found dead there and her guests being robbed," Karen offers.

I hold up my hand. "Wait. Paul was there before any of that stuff happened. So why the story about an article being written?"

No one has an answer. Why would Harriet lie to Arthur if she's planning on going with him? What was the plan for Katherine before her death? Was she going to England too, or being left on her own? Was Arthur speaking to Harriet when he talked about the 'fresh start'?

"Has there been any interest in buying the inn?" Karen asks.

A sly smile crosses Paul's lips when he replies. "Harriet asked Mario to. Mario said that Harriet thinks he could do it after he sells his mother's costume shop. Mario tells her he is working on a loan, then laughs, and says that she would be *stupida* to think he would."

Karen's eyes flash. "That's cruel."

Paul throws up his hands. "That's Mario. He is mean and has been since we were children. Arielle is afraid of him. He would boast that when babysitting her, he would snap a belt in her face, saying that if she did not do what he wanted he would use it on her. She told her mother once, but Anna did not believe her. Arielle's favorite stuffed animal was found cut to pieces with a scissors stuck in the head."

Karen covers her mouth, not able to reply. I'm sure she's thinking the same thing I am. Mario's a sociopath. No wonder Arielle didn't fight back when he was yelling at her after Anna died.

My elbows on the table, I lean forward. "So, is he selling the shop?"

"That is the best joke." Lorenzo laughs and waves his finger. "In her will, Anna left the shop to Arielle and the house to Mario. Paul took the pictures, and the house is for sale. Mario forced Arielle to move out. Now she must live in the shop."

What a jerk to his own sister! Karen's eyes fill with tears. Neither of us can understand this level of cruelty.

"Mario is selling the house, and Dani's selling the pharmacy, so when they get married, they'll have a lot of money," I comment.

A sarcastic whisper comes from Karen. "I wonder how long Dani will survive that marriage?"

That's a frightening thought. I'm sure that Mario didn't kill his mother, but he may have been willing to let someone else do it. But again, Katherine or Dani or Harriet may have done the deed on their own. Great! I can't eliminate anyone from the suspect pool. Karen's right, this situation is a mess, and we still don't know if the thefts are related or if they're a separate crime group.

"Lorenzo, have you heard any more about the burglaries?" I ask.

He sits back in his chair. "*Sì*. Two more." He holds up two fingers. "I have a . . . how you . . . crime speaker to me?"

"An informant?"

"An informant, *sì*, who says that it is a serious group. They get information on who has nice jewelry, when people will be out of their house, then they break in, steal what they can, and send it to the U.S."

"The U.S.? Where in the U.S.?"

His fingers tap the table. "New York."

CHAPTER 18

New York! This city has come up far too much with this situation to be a coincidence. Does that mean Teresa and/or Amata are part of the jewelry thefts? Are John and Linda not actually victims but part of this too? What about Harriet and Arthur? They could easily be a front for the stolen items to be transported from Venice to New York. Caputo needs to be aware.

I excuse myself to call Caputo and let him know what I've learned. I do feel bad for suggesting that airport security thoroughly check John's and Linda's bags for jewelry or even individual gems. He chuckles at my suspicious opinion of my fellow lodgers, but agrees with me, especially as they didn't notify the police of their plans to leave.

Back inside, Karen's eyes are wide open as Paul talks. What did I miss?

She shifts her gaze to me. "Dan, Paul just said that Sophia was fired by Harriet."

"Who?" I ask, directing my question more to Karen.

"The maid at the bed-and-breakfast. Harriet called her Joanna."

"Ohh. Why was she fired?"

Paul quickly divulges, "Harriet stated that she saw Sophia

in the drawer where Katherine kept her vaping cartridges. She insists that Sophia poisoned Katherine, so she fired her and reported it to the police. Both women were interviewed by the police, but no charges were pressed."

"Did Harriet give a reason that Sophia would want to poison Katherine?" I ask Paul.

"Harriet swears that Sophia was stealing. Katherine caught her and threatened to go to the police, so instead she poisoned her."

I roll my eyes. This sounds like someone is either looking for a target to blame or is deflecting blame.

A text from Caputo notifies me that John and Linda were detained at the airport. Security tore their luggage apart and found nothing. Apparently, both were upset but allowed to continue onto their flight.

Mixed feelings flood in. Part of me believes they're innocent, and yet I'm suspicious of their possible involvement in the thefts. Or did they learn something about Arthur or Harriet and decide to leave before being drawn into a murder investigation?

Karen and I finish our drinks and decide to share a portion of lasagna. Lorenzo and Paul also order dinner. Talk moves away from suspects and the investigation to Paul's other favorite topic: soccer. My eyes glazed over while he provides stats on various players, I'm at risk of falling asleep when my phone buzzes in my pocket. I pull it out and see a text that immediately gets me to my feet I fist bump the air.

All eyes in the restaurant are on me. "I just received great news from Caputo," I say.

Karen claps. "He's found the murderer!" She looks at me with a smile.

"No, better. He's captured Dr. Virk."

"How? Where?" she asks.

"He didn't give me the details." The message informed me that Virk is being detained at the police station. I want to run there right now, but it's late, and I doubt he'll escape this time. I notify Caputo that Karen and I'll be at his office in the morning to identify if it's truly Virk this time.

We finish our dinner, say good night to our companions, and walk back to the inn. The sounds of Carnival are sweeter now that justice will finally prevail and Virk will answer for his crimes in France.

The bed is soft and inviting, but doubts linger, causing me to toss and turn. Karen reaches over to touch my chest.

"Dan, either get up or lay still. You bounce me awake every time you flop over."

"Sorry. My mind won't shut down. I'm anxious about whether or not we have Virk in custody or if it's another person."

Karen softly rubs my arm. "I hear what you're saying, but being awake at 2:00 a.m. isn't going to change who's in custody."

I release a deep sigh. "You're right." I squeeze her hand. "So, have you had any dreams about this situation? Your last one was spot-on."

"No dreams so far."

That statement causes a calm to come over me. I breathe deeply, focus on seeing Virk in custody, and allow my mind to settle before falling asleep.

Both of us are up early and head down to breakfast. We're the only two. I guess murder is bad for business. Without saying a word, Harriet drops off a pot of coffee before heading back into the kitchen. We pass it off to the chaos that's occurred recently.

"I wonder how she's coping with everything? The loss of her daughter, firing the maid, putting this place on the market, guests leaving, dealing with Arthur . . ." Karen says quietly, looking at me.

I'm about to answer when Harriet is back with two full English breakfasts. I find I'm ravenous. The thought of finally being face-to-face with Virk brings me immense joy. We hurry through breakfast, leaving no leftovers, then head over to the police station. He meets us in the lobby and escorts us to the interview room.

"How did you find him?" I ask.

"We had put out a notice to watch for him. The night clerk at the hotel where he was staying called."

When we arrive, Virk is already seated at the table with shackles on his wrists and ankles. I know that face, especially those dark, emotionless eyes of his.

We make eye contact as Karen, Caputo, and I sit opposite him. A sanctimonious smirk crosses his lips. I resist the impulse to reach over and slap it off his face. Caputo signals the officer in the room to step out.

"Good to see you again," Virk says with all the warmth of a cobra.

I can't help but smile and reply, "Good to see you in custody."

He throws up his hands and shrugs, rattling his chains. "Eh."

Caputo breaks in. "Enough with reminiscing. Is it Saeed Virk, or Skanda Vita, or, should I say, Samee Virik, as that's the name on the passport you used to enter Italy?"

"Is that what I'm here for? Issues with my passport?" Virk contends.

"No," I snap, rising out of my chair. "It's your involvement in the deaths that occurred in France."

Virk shakes his head. "I have no idea what you're speaking of."

I'm about to say more when Caputo holds up his hand in front of me. "We will get to the reasons you are here. First, you entered the country illegally using a false passport, then there was the threat to Dan and Karen in their room, then there is the question of your level of involvement in several murders here in Venice, and finally the issues from the situation in France. The French authorities have expressed an interest in speaking with you. I informed them last night that you were in custody."

Virk gives a low chuckle. "First, my passport has my legal name on it. I have dual citizenship. I used my original passport from Pakistan as my Canadian passport has my name wrong," he says.

I lean forward. "You were going by Virk in France. Why if the passport was wrong?"

"I couldn't find mine from Pakistan, so I used my Canadian one. Besides, we were using noms de plume for the murder mystery game." He crosses his arms over his chest. "Second, I never threatened you here or anywhere. It won't be my handwriting on the note."

Fear washes over me. Katherine! She could've easily written it and left it in our room. I can't believe I didn't think of that.

"I have no involvement with any murders here or anywhere," he continues.

My nostrils flare. "That's a lie. You were solely responsible for the deaths of Sue Jannsen and Camille Bres."

He leans back in his chair, fingertips pressed together. "Prove it. Fingerprints on anything? DNA? Eyewitnesses? No, I didn't think so."

Caputo jumps in. "Well, all the same, the French authorities are sending a couple of officers with extradition papers. You will be turned over to them, returned to France, and will need to answer their questions regarding multiple deaths. So, we will wait for those officers, unless there is something you wish to confess to here, such as crimes you committed while in Italy."

Fear flickers in Virk's eyes. I can't wait to see him handed over to the French. I wonder if Karen and I'll be called to appear in French court.

"I have nothing to say or confess to," Virk says defiantly.

Caputo stands and taps on the door, and the officer opens it. He motions for the officer to take charge of the prisoner. Virk stands up and bows to me. Again, I quell the desire to smack him, and instead relish the sight of him being returned to a holding cell.

Once Virk is gone, Caputo sits back down, his lips pressed into a hard line. "You do know that Virk is right about having no evidence to link him to any of the murders or burglaries."

I nod. "He's smart. He'd make sure he didn't do anything

to connect him directly. I'm confident he's doing something while in Venice, and it's not vacationing."

Caputo's phone vibrates on the table. He reads the message. "The French authorities are here. I need to complete the paperwork and transfer custody. You are free to go."

I shake Caputo's hand and thank him for his hard work in making this arrest happen. As I turn to leave, I add, "Thank you for letting us be a part of this. It feels right that Virk answer in a court of law, even after all this time."

"*Prego*," Caputo replies with a wink. He accompanies us out the front door, where two gendarmes in full uniform are standing.

"The French uniforms haven't changed since I ran into them while I was in the army and training in France."

Karen snickers. "Ran into, or is it from?"

"Ha, ha." I grab her hand as we exit the police station. I'm happy about being here. For the first time, I feel like we're on the right path to solve these crimes. We just need one break in the other cases.

CHAPTER 19

"I'd like to buy you lunch," I announce.

Karen smiles at me. "Well, that would be delightful, kind sir. Where shall we dine? Venice is open to us," she says with a grand sweep of her hand.

"Let us explore, my fair maiden."

We make our way back to the inn, then walk away from the Grand Canal in as much of a straight line as Venice will allow. Several blocks later, Karen leads us into an alleyway. The first door on our left is a small bistro named The Verona.

The interior is dark and cozy. One small room to the right holds six tables. The kitchen is to the left. A quintessential Italian grandmother appears from behind a swinging door. She holds up two fingers. Karen nods. She motions for us to follow her, then seats us at a small, dark wooden table at the far end of the room. Only one other table is occupied with two patrons.

We look over our menus. A young girl with black hair, deep black eyes, and olive skin approaches our table. "What do you like?"

The grandmother returns and places plates filled with

warm bread slices, cloves of peeled garlic, and olive oil in front of each of us.

Karen orders fettuccine Alfredo, and I ask for the cheese ravioli. As we sip glasses of water and start on the bread, my phone chimes with a text message from Caputo. He reports that Virk has been handed over to the French authorities and is on his way to the airport to be deported.

"Cheers," I say, raising my glass. Karen clinks hers against mine. The tension relaxes from my shoulders, and I sit back in my chair and release a calming breath. We finish off the bread as our entrees arrive.

My first bite is amazing. Rich tomato sauce with just the slightest spicy heat, and warm cheese centers wrapped in perfect al dente pasta. Karen twirls her fork and pulls up strands of noodles with bits of Parmesan and cooked egg in a white cream sauce.

"Yum. This is great," Karen says, wiping her mouth with her napkin.

"So is mine. Want a bite?"

"No thanks. I'm good."

The rest of the meal is eaten in silence as we finish. The waitress takes away empty dishes.

"Let's have spumoni for dessert," Karen suggests.

"What's spumoni?"

"It's a type of gelato with three different flavors, nuts, and candied fruit."

I feel so happy at this moment that I can't resist. The waitress brings us one bowl with heaping scoops and two spoons.

I'm scraping the last of the dessert from the bottom of the

bowl when my phone rings with a call from Caputo. The day is going so well, I'm hoping for more good news. Possibly the capture of a murderer or burglar.

"My voice is chipper until I hear what he has to say. "NO!" I snap louder than I meant to. I can't believe what he's saying. Karen looks at me with her brow furrowed.

"How could this have happened?" I ask into the phone as I place it on speaker mode.

Caputo explains. "You're not going to believe it, because I can't. Virk has escaped. The two French officers we saw at the station weren't the real ones. I think that Virk had arranged for imposters to arrive with what looked like official paperwork to transfer custody. Virk was released to them, but thirty minutes later, two official French officers showed up with the real paperwork. Unfortunately, by that time, Virk had disappeared again. I have no idea where he is."

I take in what he's saying and try to process it. I should have known it was too easy. Virk always as a fallback plan. I hang up with Caputo and explain to Karen what happened.

Karen reaches for my hand. "Oh, Dan. I'm so sorry."

What does this mean? Is Karen in danger? Are we both? I rub my forehead.

She reads my mind. "You know he's left Italy. He's not going to take the chance of being caught again."

Where would he have gone?

"Dan!"

My head pops up, and I realize that I've been ignoring Karen while I obsess about Virk getting away.

"I'm sorry. I wasn't listening."

Karen sighs. "I was saying that as annoying as the Virk situation is, there are other people affected by what's going on here. I'd like to stop in and see how Arielle's doing at the costume shop since her mother's funeral."

I reply with little enthusiasm. "Okay."

Lunch paid for, we make our way to the shop. The bell overhead announces our arrival. Arielle emerges from the back.

"Hello," she says. "Do you need something, *signora*?"

Karen shakes her head. "I just wanted to check on you. How're you doing?"

"Fine" is her quiet answer. A tan pug wanders out from the back room.

"Who is this cute little one?" Karen asks, bending down for the dog to smell her hand.

Ariel looks at the dog and smiles. "She is Rosa. My friend and guard dog, now that I am here alone."

I'm about to ask more about Rosa when the shop door bangs open and in walk Mario and Dani. Arielle takes a step back, nearly stepping on Rosa, who's hiding behind her. So much for a guard dog.

Mario's dressed in an impeccably tailored gray pinstripe suit. His eyes flash for a moment until he realizes that Arielle is not alone. He bows in our direction, then snaps something in Italian at Arielle. Both head to the back of the shop. Dani has a smug smile on her face. She's wearing a navy-blue form-fitting dress with long sleeves, black fishnet stockings, black patent leather spiked heels, diamond teardrop earrings, and a diamond brooch.

The voices get louder in the back room. I push through

the curtain to find Mario inches from his sister's face, yelling. She's seated cringing on a wooden stool. His head snaps up when I appear.

"This is family business, not yours," Mario announces in a loud voice.

"Well, my wife and I are customers and need some assistance. Your *business* will need to wait. You could have a seat and wait until we're done."

Mario turns, his eyes flashing with anger, and heads for me. If he wants a fight, I'm up for it. I dislike bullies. He instead tries to shoulder-bump me, but I'm ready and push back, knocking him off balance. He stumbles and puts his hand on the wall to steady himself. I smirk when he looks at me, a deep red flush on his face. He says something in Italian. I'm not sure if it's meant for Dani or Arielle, but he stomps from the shop, Dani following behind.

Karen hugs Arielle, who's crying.

"I . . . am . . . sorry . . . *signore . . . e . . . signora*." Arielle sobs between breaths. "He is very sad about our *madre* dying."

That is not the emotion I was expecting her to say.

She continues, "He is selling our house and wants me to sell the shop. He thinks this will be better for me."

Karen rubs Arielle's back. "Does he always get so angry?"

Arielle shrugs. "He is passionate. He wants to travel more. Danielle is selling many of her things to be with him . . . her *farmacia*, her mother's jewelry, her house. Mario is taking care of me. I am not smart in business like him." She looks around the room. "I cannot sell now. I see, hear, and feel my mother's spirit here."

I sigh, releasing the tension in my upper body. "Arielle, is there anything Karen or I can do to help?"

She shakes her head. "No, this time of the year I am busy, and it helps. I have a few more customers coming this week and some dresses to repair. Rosa is keeping me company. I talk to her."

"Okay." Karen pats Arielle's hand. "We'll leave for now, but I'll give you our cell phone numbers. Please call if you need anything." When Arielle nods, Karen continues, "I'm very excited to go to the ball at Casa de Inglese and wear the dress you made for me. It is beautiful. I will always appreciate you and your mother's hard work."

Arielle replies with a weak smile.

"Good night for now," I call out as Karen and I head for the door. Arielle locks it behind us.

Out of sight of the shop, Karen turns to me. "Mario is such a jerk. He's so mean to Arielle, and she's so nice."

I totally agree.

Karen hooks her arm in mine. "Let's walk some. The weather is beautiful, music is playing, people are laughing, and I want to enjoy this time."

We meander along the canal until we reach Piazza San Marco. An outside table at Caffè Florian and coffee for two while a four-piece string band plays. Karen holds my hand, gently swaying to the rhythm of the music. This is people-watching at its finest. I chuckle at the thought of these colorfully dressed figures as human confetti. A rainbow of swirling, moving characters. I'm still on alert and scan the crowd for Virk. Daylight slowly fades and twilight descends as the band stops playing.

Karen stands up and reaches her hand out for me. "I suggest a slow evening walk along the canal until we find a bar and toast the night."

I take her hand. She snuggles into me as we stroll to the water. The tension in my shoulders and back returns as my coppy senses are up. Is Virk here, following us, waiting to strike? The steady waves striking the seawall calm me. Music and laughter filter down from the second floor of one of the buildings. White lights twinkle in each window of the apartment. Someone's having a party. I smile to myself.

I pull Karen closer, the warmth of her body radiating to me. Even at this time of the evening, the streets are busy with people. A strong smell of roses catches my nose as a dark figure crashes into me. The blow knocks Karen down with a thud as she lands on the ground. I'm propelled backward a few steps when a raised arm before me holds some type of weapon about to strike me. I raise my arm to deflect the item, then turn to grab it. I manage to foot sweep the attacker and push them. The person staggers back, catches their heel, and falls back into the canal. A shout is followed by a splash.

Karen brushes herself off as she stands up. "Are you alright?" she asks me.

"Yes. What about you?"

"Fine. Luckily I landed on my butt and back but didn't hit my head."

"*Aiutami*" bellows up from the water. I turn on my phone flashlight to find who's in the water. It's Mario!

My first thought is to leave him there. I extend my hand to him, but the water sucks him under and I lose sight of him. I move the flashlight from side to side until he reappears on the surface, thrashing and screaming, "*No. No. Aiutami*!" A single red rose bloom floats nearby. He takes my hand, and I pull him up. He's muttering in Italian and shaking as he sits on the walkway.

Karen taps my back. "I called Caputo. He's on his way over."

I stand guard over Mario to prevent his escape when several emergency workers appear. Two tend to Mario with blankets and check his vitals. Caputo walks over and looks at me. "You two okay?"

I nod.

He kneels next to Mario, who continues to speak, but I don't understand any of it. Caputo pats him on the shoulder before standing and coming to talk to Karen and me.

"Mario is praying for protection," he says. "He is saying that a skeleton of a woman in a lace dress and a silver scarf grabbed him and pulled him under the water. He saw her skull with white teeth facing him. She had a red rose on the shoulder of her dress, and he smelled roses while under water." Caputo chuckles and shakes his head. "I do not believe him."

Karen shoots me a sideways glance and utters, "Thank you, Sofia."

"I'll be pressing charges for attempted assault," I tell Caputo. "It'll be a good reason to question him further about the murders and burglaries."

He shakes my hand. "Please follow me to my office."

The emergency workers have Mario on his feet, wrapped in a blanket, until Caputo places handcuffs on him.

CHAPTER 20

At the police station, we wait for Mario to be processed and brought to the interview room. Karen and I have given our statements as to what happened. We don't mention our belief that Sofia, the ghost of the canal, saved us. Mario shuffles into the room dressed in a prisoner's jumpsuit with shackles on his ankles and wrists, his arrogance deflated.

Caputo glares, crossing his arms over his chest. "Here is the plan that Dan is offering," he says.

"Deal," I correct him.

Caputo furrows his brow.

"Here's the 'deal.'"

"*Sì, sì.* Deal." He focuses on Mario with no humor in his eyes. "You tell us what you know about the murders of your mother, Katherine, and Andrea. Also, anything you know about the burglaries. If you are truthful and helpful, Dan and Karen will drop the charges of assault. You lie or are not completely truthful, then you will be charged. *Capire?*"

Mario nods slowly without enthusiasm.

"We will start with Anna's death," Caputo states, turning on a tape recorder. "What do you know?"

"I do not know anything. I was not in Italy when *mia madre* was killed."

"You thought that Katherine killed Anna, so you killed her," I state.

"No, but I think Katherine did it. She was a crazy girl. She would get very mad if she did not get what she wanted."

Caputo looks at Mario. "What about Harriet? You lied to her about wanting to buy the inn."

Mario shakes his head. "I led Harriet to believe that Dani and I would buy it together, but Harriet is not a nice lady. Katherine told me she planned to kill Arthur so Harriet would get all of his money. Sell Casa de Inglese and get that money, too. I think Katherine was then going to kill her *madre* so she would be very rich. She asked for money after *mia madre* died."

I jump in. "So, you killed Katherine when you found out she killed your mother."

A red flush erupts on Mario's face. "No. I did not kill Katherine. I did not like her, but not enough to kill her."

"She used the poison you brought back from one of your trips to South America to kill Anna. The poison dart frog venom," I say to him.

He violently shakes his head. "Katherine asked for the special poison because her mother wanted to kill rats at the inn. I would not have given it to her if I knew she would use it on *mia madre*." Mario's head is on the table, crying. "I am sorry, Mama. I did this. Forgive me."

"You want us to believe that Katherine did this all alone," I say. "You've tricked Harriet into thinking you'll buy her inn. Maybe you also tricked Katherine into believing you'd marry her, but your mother was a problem. I've seen you bully your sister. You want her shop. When you get angry, you take revenge. That's why you came after me."

His eyes flash at me. "You were in family business. You embarrassed me in front of *mia famiglia*. I will take care of my sister. That shop killed my mother. She worked so hard for very little. I do not want my sister to be an old lady with no money." He straightens up in his chair. "I have a buyer for the shop."

Karen asks if anyone else knew about Katherine's plan to kill Arthur. Mario shrugs and shakes his head.

Caputo focuses on Mario. "What do you know about the death of Andrea?"

"I had nothing to do with that or the burglaries."

My mind is trying to piece together these cases, but they still seem unrelated.

Caputo instructs an officer to return Mario to his cell. Mario hangs his head as he exits the room. "Well, do you believe him?" Caputo asks us.

I lift my hands in surrender. "I guess. I just can't see a motive. Mario doesn't appear to have wanted his mother dead. He could have killed Katherine if he believed she killed Anna, but are we sure that Katherine did kill her?"

Karen is drumming her fingers on the table.

"What do you think?" I ask her.

She sets her lips in a line determinately. "This is a different spin on it. Katherine killed Anna, but not for herself. She could've done it for Dani, her friend, and Mario to be together and buy the inn. Once the inn is sold, her mother has the money, then Harriet and Arthur move back to England, where Arthur 'dies,' leaving her mother even more money. She has the poison, she could kill Arthur at any time once he inherits, right? If that scenario works, it's a matter to find out who had motive to kill Katherine. Arthur moves to the top of my list," she says, raising her eyebrows, looking between Caputo and me.

Caputo throws down his pen. I agree with the sentiment that we don't have one clear suspect.

"Have you checked everyone's phone records?" I ask.

"*Sì*. No unusual activity by anyone. In the weeks and days before each death, none of our suspects had calls that were out of their normal call history. No strange numbers or connections to people they had not called before."

"What about the number of suspects that have traveled to or plan to travel to New York?" Karen adds.

Caputo sighs, then motions for us to follow him. In his office, he pulls papers from a file. "Amata recently visited family she has there. And Teresa has been offered the head chef position at a restaurant in New York. She also filed for divorce from Andrea, six weeks ago. A court date had been set. I interviewed her. She stated that Andrea planned to buy her half of the building that included the restaurant and the living space above."

"And we know that John and Linda went there for vacation and nothing illegal," I say with a wince. "My bad."

Karen asks, "So when does Teresa need to start her new job? And has she put the restaurant here up for sale? Andrea didn't sound like he was selling. If she put it on the market before Andrea died, then she planned to kill him."

Caputo scribbles a note before pulling another file. "Here

is the autopsy on Andrea. Poison. Arsenic in the contents of his stomach."

Karen's eyes widen. "It's a good thing neither of us liked his choice in wine."

"I'm interested in who removed the bottle with the remains of the wine, the glasses, and all other evidence," I say. "Karen and I saw Andrea cut the seal on the bottle, so if the poison was in the wine, it had to be induced by a syringe through the cork. So, either it was the same person, or they had an accomplice."

"A full search of the restaurant, garbage, and surrounding area provided many empty wine bottles, glasses, and things. All were tested, and no poison was found," Caputo states.

"My bet is that all the evidence is at the bottom of the canal," Karen comments.

Caputo and I look at her with surprise.

She adds, "Well, it would've been easy to just drop everything in while we were focused on Andrea."

Caputo lets out a long sigh and leans back in his chair. I'm impressed with how my wife's mind works. It's a perfectly simple solution to dispose of the evidence.

"I will get a dive team to try and recover the bottle and glasses." Caputo extends his hand, which I shake. Karen and I are free to leave.

Once we're outside, Karen grabs my arm. "Let's call Paul and set up the walking tour. I feel like walking and seeing this amazing city would be good for us.

I dial his number. He says that he can be ready in an hour and to meet him at Piazza San Marco. We stroll from the police station to the piazza, get a cup of coffee, and wait for Paul.

Lorenzo spots us and joins us at our table. "Mario has been arrested for trying to assault you. Are you both alright?"

I laugh. "Yes to all of the above."

"What can you tell me about his arrest?" Lorenzo pulls a tape recorder from his pocket and leans his elbows on the table.

"He attempted to hit me with something, but I was able to fight back, and he fell into the canal."

"Why did he attack you?"

I throw up my hands. "I'm not really sure. I never got an answer."

"Are the *polizia* investigating if he killed Anna, Katherine, and Andrea?"

"You would need to ask Caputo about that. Karen and I just reported the attempted assault." Not the whole truth, but not a complete lie.

He eyes me suspiciously. I know he wants more information, but I won't compromise an ongoing investigation.

Paul arrives. "Hello, all. *Signore e signora*. Are you ready to walk?"

Karen and I reply enthusiastically in unison, "Yes!"

I extend my hand to Lorenzo and wish him a good day.

Paul sweeps his arm toward the buildings in front of us. The homes and businesses blend in a harmonious rainbow. "Venezia is the capital of the Veneto region. It is built on a group of 126 islands, which are connected by 472 bridges. Approximately 521,000 people live in the historic part of Venice. Venice comes from the Venti people that lived here in the tenth century B.C. It was the capital of the Republic of Venice from 810 to 1797 and was a major financial and maritime power during the Middle Ages and the Renaissance. It was a center of trade in silk, grain, spice, and art."

Paul is walking, talking, and hopefully will take us back to the inn. With the twists and turns he's taking, I'm completely lost.

"Are the buildings here original to when Venice was built?" Karen asks, looking up and around at the various buildings and their colorful facades.

Paul replies with a sigh. "It is hard to tell as there are no surviving records on that. Venice has been invaded several times by waves of Germanic and Hun invaders. Napoleon came to Venice in 1797." He goes on about the twelve founding families tracing their family line to Rome, and also mentions the doges and how the word "doge" in Venetian translates to "leader."

While Paul continues the tour, my attention is caught as we walk past the front window of Dani's pharmacy. She's behind the counter with Arthur in front of her. His neck is flaming red, and he's leaning on the counter with his face inches from hers. She looks up and sees that I'm watching, then taps Arthur. He turns and waves to me, then exits the store.

"Everything alright in there?" I ask, looking between him and Dani, who avoids my eye contact.

"Yes, yes. Just fine, old man. I was giving that girl a piece of my mind. She called to say that Harriet's prescription was ready. I come all the way over here, then she says it won't be ready until tomorrow. Wasted trip, I say."

"That's too bad."

"Well, must get on. Things to do. Good seeing you again." He wanders off and disappears around the corner.

I turn around and can't find Karen or Paul. I scan the area until I see Karen, who's four stores in front of me. She's looking at me with her hands on her hips. I hurry to catch up.

A scowl covers her face. "What were you doing?"

"I'll tell you later."

Paul is slightly ahead of us, and we continue the tour. He talks about the artists that lived in the city, but I'm not listening. Something about the interaction between Dani and Arthur was far more intense than a simple mix-up about the readiness of a prescription. It looked more like he was threatening her, but why?

The continued traversing through the city, up and over bridges, and general being on my feet has my knees screaming for me to stop and sit.

I raise my hand as Paul is speaking about St. Mark's Basilica and how the original entrance was that of the Hippodrome of Constantinople that was plundered in 1204.

"I'm sorry, but my legs are hurting, and I need a break. Is there somewhere we can sit and maybe have a drink?"

Paul knits his brows together. I'm sure most of his tourists complete his tour without complaint. "*Sì, Sì*. There is a place I know. Follow me."

He leads us to a small restaurant tucked in an alley, finds a table outside and excuses himself for another appointment he has. Karen thanks him for his time and pays him. I order a round of drinks for us. Karen pulls a couple of aspirins from her pocket, which I take along with the beer I ordered. Karen orders a caprese salad for us to share along with bruschetta and bread. When the food comes, we dig in . . .

Karen turns her attention to me. "What did you see earlier that caused you to stop? It freaked me out when I couldn't find you."

I explain the scene between Dani and Arthur at the pharmacy. "I didn't believe Arthur's explanation of why he was angry."

"Did you hear anything he was saying?" Karen whispers, leaning closer to me.

"No."

"Arthur can be a bit wacky. What if it's early onset dementia? He could be prone to outbursts over little things."

She could be right, but my coppy senses tell me there's more to this situation.

Karen and I finish our drinks and head back to the inn. As we step into the hall, Harriet comes out of the library. She stops when she sees us. "Oh, it's you two." Her disappointment is evident.

"Sorry to let you down," I chuckle. "Who were you expecting?"

"I can't seem to find Arthur. The bloody man," she snaps.

"He went to the pharmacy to pick up your medication, but it wasn't ready just yet," I inform her. "He seemed upset by that."

"Well, that's not possible. I don't take any medication," Harriet replies. "You completely misunderstood what he was saying." She turns and moves toward the kitchen.

Karen looks at me. "Dan, why would Arthur make up a story about being at the pharmacy to pick up her medication?"

I scratch my chin. "He lied about that. What else is he lying about?"

CHAPTER 21

Curiouser and curiouser. Something is going on, but I just can't figure out what.

Karen touches my arm. "I could use a nap. Want to join me?"

"I never pass up a chance for a nap." I tuck my arm through Karen's as we head up the stairs. My knees will appreciate the rest.

Upon lying down, the aching in my legs makes it impossible for me to sleep. I give up and search through the medications we have in the room.

Karen sits up. "What are you looking for?"

"Any form of pain relief."

"I don't think I have any left. We should head to the pharmacy to see what they have."

Both of us dress and walk to the pharmacy. Dani is waiting on another couple, Italian flowing back and forth between them. When she's finished, Karen approaches her. "What pain relievers are available?" Dani shows her where they are. I'm wandering up and down the aisles, looking at the shelves.

Enzo, the sports reporter that Karen and I first met at Mi Famiglia, enters. He's speaking to the couple that Dani just finished with. Karen calls me over to look at our choices, and we take two different bottles to the register.

Dani places our items in a bag while Karen leans in and whispers, "How are you doing?"

Dani knits her brow together.

"Dan saw Arthur being very angry with you," Karen says. "I hope it wasn't too upsetting."

"No, *signora*, it is fine. His medicine did not come in as I thought it would. He said he needed it today or he would not have any, but it came in now."

"I'm glad to hear it. I don't know if I told you how sorry I am at the loss of your friend, Katherine."

Dani shrugs. "*Grazie, signora*. Excuse me." She turns to take the next customer.

I'm speaking with Enzo when Karen joins us. Enzo introduces the couple as Giovanni and Bianca Gallo, an older, distinguished-looking couple. I shake hands with Giovanni, then bid them goodbye as they leave the store.

"I'm sorry. Did I interrupt your conversation?" Karen asks.

"No, No. They were here for their medicines," Enzo says. "They were telling me about their trip to Greece. They are very excited. It is their fiftieth wedding anniversary. Dani helped them get enough medicine for the whole trip. Ten days they will be gone."

Karen gushes, "What a wonderful trip. I hope they have a great time. Are they taking a cruise?"

"*Sì*," Enzo replies.

"Well, we don't want to keep you. Have a great night," I say.

"*Grazie*. I too am going on a trip to cover a soccer game that is being played in New York. I am very excited to see the city. *Arrivederci*." Enzo moves to the counter to speak with Dani.

I'm speechless. New York? Now Enzo is going there. This is too much of a coincidence. I need to talk to Caputo.

Karen and I head to Mi Famiglia for a light dinner. I intend to take the pain relievers with a drink or two. My knees are still screaming in pain.

Karen leans into me as we walk. "Dani lied when I talked to her about Arthur being angry yesterday. She said he was upset that *his* medicine wasn't ready. He said that the medicine was for Harriet, who later denied taking any medications."

"It's interesting. Maybe Arthur got mixed up and misspoke when he said the medicine was for Harriet. He can been kinda absentminded."

"True."

"Did you hear that Enzo is going to New York, too?."

Karen laughs. "Maybe we're the only people in Venice NOT going to New York. I wonder if that's where Virk is headed?"

"Don't mention that name!"

The inside of Mi Famiglia is warm and inviting, the smells of warm bread and tomato sauce drawing me in. We find a table at the back of the room and both order limoncello to start. I know I was thinking a "light" supper, but spaghetti Bolognese is calling my stomach. Karen orders the same.

"At the rate I'm eating, I'm going to gain twenty pounds on this trip," she snickers. "And enjoy every bite."

I swallow two pills, wash them down with the limoncello, and relax into my chair.

Karen is quiet.

"What are you thinking?"

Karen rubs her temples. "I can't shake the feeling of déjà vu. It's like I've seen something or experienced it before, but what is it? I just can't remember."

"When did you first feel it?"

"In the pharmacy. Those people that Enzo introduced us to . . . have we met them before? Were they at the first ball at Casa de Inglese?"

I shrug. "I don't think so. I don't remember them from the party. Maybe?"

"It'll come to me. I just hope it doesn't happen at two in the morning."

Dinner arrives, and we tuck in. The tomato sauce mingled with the perfectly cooked spaghetti is warm and satisfying. We finish every bite. At long last, the pain in my knees has diminished significantly. A second round of limoncello and a full stomach should help me nod off later when we crawl into bed.

The traditional and self medications co-mingle to ease my walk back to the inn. We sit up reading until it's time for bed. Karen and I snuggle until I drift off to sleep.

Karen calls out my name, jolting me awake. "What's wrong?" I ask.

"I figured out my déjà vu."

I look at the clock. It's not 2:00 a.m., but close. "Okay, what is it?"

"I just had a dream that the people we met at the pharmacy, the Gallos, were talking to a cat in the moonlight. When we first arrived in Venice and Lorenzo stopped at the pharmacy, people were talking to Dani about their trip and later were burglarized. Earlier, the Gallos were in the pharmacy talking about their trip and how they leave today."

"Okay. So . . . what?"

"The cat in my dream could be a cat burglar. I think Caputo should stake out the Gallos' home while they're gone. I believe with every fiber of my being that they're going to be the next victims."

"I totally trust your dreams, but, um, I'm trying to find a way to give this clue to Caputo that doesn't sound crazy. I'm not sure he'll want to act on the fact that it came to you in a dream."

Karen's laughing. "True, and we can't forget about the victims talking to a cat in the moonlight."

"Yeah, let's not forget that part." I'm laughing too. "Was it a full moon?"

"No, it was a crescent moon. Silver and shiny. Light spilling on the ground. Oh, goodness, I do sound crazy."

I let out a low snicker. "I'll call Caputo in the morning."

Karen snuggles into me and begins to breathe slowly and rhythmically. Her dream may sound crazy, but I've learned not to dismiss my wife's "gift." I just hope Caputo respects it too.

The next morning, our breakfast finishes with no conversation from Harriet, who dropped off coffee and breakfast plates without a pause. Karen told me beforehand not to ask Harriet how she's doing. If she wants to talk about the situation with us, she'll do it.

We meander our way to the police station to discuss the events to date with Caputo. In his office, Caputo sits behind his desk, fingertips pressed together, listening.

I try to "cop up" the information's credibility.

His eyes narrow. "What are you really trying to tell me?"

I lean forward in my chair, intending to clarify, when Karen grabs my arm.

"To be totally honest, the information came from me," she says. "I had a dream that contained the information Dan gave you."

Caputo's eyes widen. "So, exactly what did you see in the dream?"

While Karen relays the dream, I internally cringe.

She places her hands on the desk. "I know it sounds crazy, but my dreams have a way of coming true after a little symbolic interpretation. The clues may be disguised, but once revealed, they're accurate."

Caputo smiles and looks down. "I do not think that it is crazy. I know because I come from a long line of women who have similar gifts. People in my village went to my grandmother for help and healing. Some thought her a witch, but most thought she was wonderful. My mother has dreams and premonitions."

Karen releases a deep sigh and sits back in her chair. "I'm so happy you don't think me a lunatic."

"Let us investigate your dream. First the couple, the Gallos, were there. Now they are leaving on vacation. It is possible their home will be targeted for a robbery."

"Yes," we say in unison.

He continues, "The cat. Who do you think it is? Dani?"

"I'm not sure if she's the cat or reports to the cat," Karen says. "Cats can hold secrets. She may be the cat burglar, or knows who it is." Karen looks between me and Caputo.

I agree." I keep thinking there's more to it than I remember. It may be that most burglaries are committed at night, so the moon would be out."

"Also, to be honest, I have always suspected that Dani has secrets," Caputo remarks. "I do not know what they are. Just like a cat never lets you know what they are thinking, but you know they are." He smiles. "Thank you for the information. I hope you are wrong about the Gallos being possible victims, but I will see about doing surveillance on their home. Also, on another note, divers found a wine bottle, glasses, and plates that were dumped in the canal after Andrea was murdered. They are all at the lab to be tested for poison and fingerprints."

I hang my head. "You know that if any prints are found they could belong to Karen and me."

Caputo chuckles. "Yes, I do know that."

Before we leave, I let him know about Enzo and his upcoming trip to New York. Caputo nods in acknowledgement. I shake his hand, as does Karen.

As we walk away from the station, Karen takes my hand. "I feel good about that meeting. I was nervous that he'd think I'm a nut. He's very open-minded, which reminds me of you when you were a detective."

"Thank you. That's nice of you to say."

We decide to take a walk to the San Polo neighborhood. However, walking is a challenge with the number of people on the street, so after pictures at the Rialto Bridge, we head to Gelatoteca Suso—the gelato experience of Venice. The shop is bright and airy, with sunlight streaming through the large glass windows as we step inside. Mouthwatering flavors fill the cases.

"What do think about Madagascar?" I ask Karen. "It sounds exotic."

"Dan, it's vanilla. Madagascar vanilla."

"That's disappointing. What are you having?"

"I'm deciding between Tango, which has cappuccino ice cream, caramel swirls, and cocoa crumble, or Cheese Tart, which has cheesecake ice cream, caramel crumble, and a raspberry sauce. I think I'll go with Tango."

"Both sound great. I'm having Opera, which has hazelnut ice cream and is covered with a hazelnut spread."

I order a dish of each. We sit outside, savoring this treat, and people-watch. I must admit, I still have a bit of a nervous reaction when I see a plague doctor costume and hope it isn't Virk. When we finish, Karen suggests we take a boat ride up and down the Grand Canal. We purchase tickets for the vaporetto, settle into the wooden seats, and watch the city roll by.

"I'm not hungry, so can we skip dinner tonight?" Karen asks me.

"That ice cream filled me up, so I'm good."

The ride is calm and enjoyable, a combination of people-watching, listening to the street music, and smelling the various restaurants. We pick out our favorite houses along the canal and speculate about who lives there.

We pass a large yellow residence. "I think it's a long-lost relative to the Medici family," Karen says. "He's hoping to capitalize on the family name for a new business venture here in Venice."

I point to a five-story, deep-orange building. "The person living in that house is an international spy. She's enjoying a rest after a difficult case of discovering the true identity of a double agent."

"Oh, I like to idea that the spy is a she. Very Black Widow."

"What is the new business venture for the Medici family?"

Karen releases a deep laugh. "A water park, of course."

"That's perfect. I wish him the best of luck with that idea."

We continue to speculate on what's behind the walls of these houses, getting more outrageous as we go. Karen picks a small two-story white house and says it's the home of a secret clown collection. She comments that her niece, Lisa, would never go in there due to Lisa's dislike of clowns. I suggest it could be a doll collection, which would bother our grand-daughter, Hannah, who fears dolls, especially those that look back at you. The evening passes with laughter and joy, and the vaporetto returns us to a stop near the inn. Karen and I walk home holding hands.

CHAPTER 22

Karen and I finish our evening watching television in bed in our room. She flips through the stations until she finds a movie she likes that's in English: *Strangers on a Train*.

"I don't think I know that one," I say.

"It's an Alfred Hitchcock movie. Two strangers meet on a train, start talking about exchanging murders. One man wants his wife killed while the other man wants his father dead. So, the first guy will kill the other man's father, and the second man will kill the first guy's wife. Then each can establish an alibi, and they have no other connection to one another since they're strangers. It's a great psychological thriller."

"Okay. Let's do that."

We settle in to watch. Sleep takes me over before the end of the movie.

The next morning, I wake on the edge of the bed just as my phone rings. It's Caputo with a report that surveillance on the Gallo home turned up nothing. No attempted burglary. I thank him for the update. I get ready to head down to breakfast.

Harriet is once again a twirling top, spinning through the dining room with coffee and breakfast plates.

We finish and head back to our room. Karen enters the

hallway just outside it and stops so suddenly that I bump into her.

"What's wrong?" I ask as I look around for what caught her attention.

"My déjà vu. I feel like I saw something or heard something here."

"Just now?"

Karen turns to me. "No. The memory is almost there." She shakes her head. "Ugh, this is so frustrating. I can't remember at this point."

I pat her on the back, and we continue up to our room. Karen lays out the gifts she has so far, then makes a list of items she still needs to pick up.

We decide to walk and shop for the items before this evening's grand ball. We start down the stairs when we notice Harriet decorating the balcony by herself. The bunting in navy-blue and silver is not cooperating. Karen hurries to help secure one end.

Harriet's eyes flash with anger when she looks at Karen. "I don't expect my *guest* to help with preparations in my house. Thank you, but I can manage nicely at this time. I've hired additional staff to help later today."

Karen mouths, "Okay," and joins me on the stairs as we make our way outside.

"That was rude," I comment to Karen.

She shakes her head. "I can appreciate that she's under pressure while mourning her daughter, but wow, what an ice queen."

Window-shopping fills part of our day until we come

upon a costumer's shop other than Arielle's. Karen stops, then moves closer to the window. She points. "That's it."

I survey the contents of the window display. "What's it?"

"That!" She points with emphasis. "That silver mask with the crescent moon and snake accents. Now, who was wearing it?"

I'm not sure what we're talking about, but I wouldn't dare interrupt her now. I can practically see the wheels turning in her mind. Eyes closed, her fingertips twitch as if she's combing through a file cabinet. This is a memory file.

Her head snaps up. "Dani."

"Dani . . . what?"

"The night of Harriet's first ball. Dani was wearing a silver mask with a crescent moon on one side and a snake on the other. I remember now, because she was friendly with Caputo, I was shocked when I realized the snake was close to his face. Caputo had a sly grin when she left him." Karen ponders this thought before continuing. "I wonder if they are or have been involved with each other. He seemed comfortable with her touch."

"So, is Dani the cat?" I ask.

"I don't know. I'm questioning if we can trust Caputo. Is he involved, and that's why no one has been caught? Or is Dani using him for updates on the investigation?"

"My coppy senses tell me he's a good, honest cop. I think we risk it and trust him."

I pull out my phone and update him on Karen's recall. He scoffs at the idea that Dani's the burglar but concedes she may be a source of information to the thief. I ask if he's been invited to the grand ball at Casa de Inglese. He confirms he has but may need to skip it and continue the surveillance on the Gallo home. We discuss a plan that he attends the ball, make his presence known, and still have a team watching the house. Hopefully this is an open invitation for the burglar to try entering the Gallo home. He agrees.

I'm excited at the thought of a possible resolution to these thefts, much happier than I have been for the last few days. The thief might be Virk, and he'd be caught again! I know it's not my case, but being part of a potential solution still feels good, if this works.

We continue to browse different shops. Karen finds a few small things to buy, then we make our way back to the inn. Harriet is in the hall, directing several people to the placement of tables, chairs, decorations, and service utensils. We move our way through and up the stairs to our room.

"I know this trip has been difficult at times, but I'm excited about the ball tonight," Karen says enthusiastically.

"Me too, and if we're lucky, the burglar will fall into the trap."

I lie back on the bed, then suddenly wake with a start. I had fallen asleep. Karen is next to me, reading.

"How do you feel at trying to sneak a peek at what's happening downstairs?

Karen snaps her book closed and smiles. We creep out of our room and look over the banister.

The transformation is awesome. The balcony is strewn with silver and blue ribbons, bunting, and bows. Tables gleam with centerpieces of tall candleholders and flowers encircling the base. I could believe in fairy dust at this very moment.

We catch angry looks from Harriet, and like naughty children withdraw from our vantage point to our room. Karen and I laugh behind the closed bedroom door.

"Harriet sure knows how to throw a party. I wonder who's providing the food now that Andrea is dead?" Karen thinks out loud.

"I don't know, but I'm sure it'll be good. And I'll eat more than I should."

Karen and I get ready to arrive downstairs on time. Karen is again in her green dress and matching gold mask with sequin scrolls and feathers at the top. She has her hair pulled into a French twist. I'm wearing black pants, a vest that matches Karen's dress, and a white shirt.

I'm taken aback at my anxiety of seeing masked people filling the room. The buffet tables are once again set up. Amata darts out from the kitchen with warming trays for the food.

Karen steps in front of her and smiles. "Hello, Amata. This looks wonderful. Are you helping?"

"*Sì, signora*. Teresa is training me to be a manager of her restaurant in New York."

"Wow, you're going to New York with Teresa? When are you leaving?"

Amata looks at the floor. "Next week. Teresa sold the restaurant and can use the money for her new place."

Karen's eyes widen. "That was fast. She found a buyer quickly."

"No, no, the buyer, he signed the papers last week. *Scusa*, I must go and finish."

Karen pauses with her mouth open for a moment, then

whispers, "This must have been planned for a while. You can't find a buyer on such short notice."

"We need to let Caputo know about this," I say. "We were told that Andrea was buying Teresa out and they were divorcing."

I look around the room until I find Caputo. He's wearing all black—shirt, pants, mask, and a long cape tied at his neck. I inform him of what Amata just relayed.

Surprise crosses Caputo's face. "I will look into it," he replies.

Harriet marches in from the kitchen in a high-waisted, long-sleeve, navy-blue and silver gown with a sparkling silver wig. Soft twinkling white lights are embedded throughout the dress. It's quite the entrance.

Karen approaches with a broad smile. "You look stunning." Harriet bows slightly.

Arthur wanders in from the library. His navy-blue and silver captain's uniform matches his wife's dress. He's wearing white stockings and silver shoes. As they stand next to each other, the couple is very captivating together.

Arthur begins adjusting trays on the buffet table.

Harriet stomps up to him. "Leave it be! Arthur, this will go much better if you only do what you're told to!"

He stutters back, "Um, very good, my dear. Must get on."

Harriet straightens the items back to the way they were before Arthur moved them. Arthur makes his way around the room, speaking to guests.

Karen and I move to a side table, where Caputo joins us. Karen looks at us both and rolls her eyes. Caputo and I are sitting with our backs to a wall, a clear view of the hall. Cops look the same in any language.

The front door flings open, and Lorenzo calls out, "*Buona sera*, all." He's wearing a white, full-length fur-trimmed coat with red pants and a red-and-gold beaded vest. His mask is white, but his headdress boasts oversized gold wings inset with smaller red wings and a center sunburst in gold and red. He clutches a gold shield in his left hand.

Harriet's mouth opens and closes without a word. I agree. What's there to say to that outfit? He sweeps through the room towards Harriet, taking her hand in both of his and kissing her on each cheek. Scarlet climbs up her neck to her face. I believe that she's extremely angry, but she says nothing. You could peel the smile off her face.

He converses with people at each table, thanking them for their comments on his outfit. He briefly stops to speak to us before moving to another table. Caputo looks as if to say something when we catch sight of Dani.

She's wearing a bell-shaped dress in rich purple with white lace at the cuffs and neckline and a matching mask. No moon or snake. She makes eye contact with me, then looks away to sit at another table. I make a mental note to check on her every thirty minutes or so. If she doesn't disappear from here, then she's not the burglar. But I still haven't ruled her out as a co-conspirator or the mastermind.

Soft, soothing music from a string quartet on the balcony fills the air. Waitstaff in black pants, white shirts, black bow ties, and plain white masks move around the room with trays holding glasses of sparkling white or red wine. I take a white wine for both Karen and myself. Caputo declines. Amata carries trays of spaghetti Bolognese and ravioli and places them in the warming trays. Bowls of salad, cold pastas, sliced meats, and breads also are arranged on the tables.

Harriet moves halfway up the staircase. "I just want to say thank you for coming this evening. Please enjoy the dinner. More wine will be coming around. Help yourselves."

While Karen and I wait for the line to thin out, I scan the room for Dani. She's nowhere to be found. I excuse myself to walk around to try and locate her. My plan is to check the kitchen first. As I step toward the kitchen, she slips out from the library and into the hall. Curiouser and curiouser. What would she be doing in there?

I do an inventory of people. Harriet, Lorenzo, and now Dani are all accounted for. Arthur is missing. Maybe this isn't his thing? I know Harriet wants him to smoke outside. I move toward the kitchen, and he nearly knocks me over. "Sorry, old man. Didn't see you there."

Okay, all of my suspects are present. My mind starts to run other scenarios for the burglaries and murders when a loud crash causes me to jump and turn around in midair. In the hall, chaos has erupted. Harriet is screaming and calling Amata a stupid girl. On the floor is an overturned pan of spaghetti. Karen runs past me into the kitchen, as does Arthur.

I move toward Amata, who has tears running down her face. Quiet sobs escape her lips. Teresa steps out from the kitchen.

Harriet is inches away from Amata's face. "Do something. Get a rag and clean this mess up."

Amata is rooted in place.

"What are you waiting for, you stupid cow?" Harriet continues.

Amata sprints to the bathroom. I assure Harriet that Karen and I will help her.

She focuses her eyes on me. "This is not your or your wife's responsibility. Apparently, it's impossible to find quality staff. Excuse me." She makes her way to the kitchen. Teresa is scooping the spaghetti and sauce into the dropped pan. I go and sit at the table. It dawns on me that Karen hasn't returned, and neither has Arthur.

"Have you noticed that several people are absent from the hall?" I ask Caputo, tapping his arm. He follows me to the kitchen.

I open the door to a horrific scene: smashed ceramic bowls on the floor, broken glassware, cutlery across multiple surfaces. Blood smeared on the countertop appears to be from Arthur, who's unconscious on the floor, blood on the side of his head. Harriet's against the counter with Karen standing inches away, pointing a knife at her. "What the heck?" I say, startled at the sight. Caputo rushes to Arthur, who groans quietly, then pulls out his phone and calls for assistance. He discards his mask and cape.

Harriet's body and voice plead for assistance while Karen's hands shake slightly but hold fast with the knife. "She attacked my husband without cause and turned that knife on me. Help me, please."

"Karen?" I ask, wanting an explanation.

"I found the head of the burglary ring," she answers with a shrug.

CHAPTER 23

I gently remove the knife from Karen's hand. "Harriet? I doubt she's the cat burglar."

Karen snaps, "Not her. Him." She points to Arthur. He groans and sits up, leaning against the cabinets. Blood trickles down his face.

Caputo secures Harriet with flex cuffs. "Karen, tell me what happened here."

Karen holds her hands to stop the shaking, speaking rapidly. "When Amata dropped the food, I ran here for something to clean it up with. I opened different drawers until I found a stack of towels. I grabbed a bunch and pulled them out. When I did, a notebook fell open on the ground, so I picked it up to put it back in the drawer, but it had notes with descriptions of jewelry, their value, and addresses. While I looked at it, I didn't hear Arthur come into the room. I jumped when I realized he was there and moved to the counter." She takes a deep breath and releases it slowly. "He said, 'I'm very sorry you found that, my dear,' then grabbed a knife and came at me. I found a frying pan and swung it, knocking the knife out of his hand. He grabbed my wrist, so I hit him in the head. Harriet came into the room at that time. I picked up the knife to hold her off until help arrived.!" She drops into a chair.

Harriet pulls away from Caputo. Her hands still bound, she runs to Arthur. "My love, are you alright?" She's kissing his face and cradling him. Karen, Caputo, and I stare at her in disbelief. We've never seen this side of Harriet with Arthur before.

Paramedics arrive and tend to Arthur. Per Caputo, they determine it's not a serious wound and he won't need transportation to the hospital. A large bandage is placed over his head.

Caputo instructs his officers to clear the hall except for Dani, Lorenzo, Teresa, and Amata. He moves us all to the library. I guess he's "rounding up the suspects." How very Agatha Christie.

Caputo stands with his hands on his hips, waiting while his officers escort people out of the hall. Before any more instructions are given, his phone rings. I don't understand what's being said.

"It is more good news," he whispers to me. "The burglar has been caught."

Surprise crosses my face. "I guess it's not Dani. Who is it?" I ask, skeptically.

He waves me off. "My team is bringing him here."

Caputo has Arthur handcuffed to a chair while everyone else takes available seats. Karen and I retrieve additional chairs from the hall, which is now quiet and vacant. The aftermath of a party interrupted looks so sad.

Two officers arrive and escort a young man into the library. He looks familiar, but I can't place him.

Karen's hand covers her mouth. "It's Marco, the boat driver."

"And Dani's cousin," Caputo adds. "He was arrested after coming out of the second-story bedroom window at the Gallo house."

Dani leaps forward and erupts into a litany of angry Italian. Marco takes a step back.

"Karen and I going to need some translation."

"Well, she said that she told Marco that it was too dangerous to break in, but he did," Caputo says. "She called him an idiot. He knew that the Gallos were away, and no one suspected him. He was right."

Karen tilts her head. "What's Arthur's involvement with the burglaries?"

"Nothing!" Arthur exclaims. "I don't know anything about this situation. Stop playing silly buggers with me."

"Liar! You know because you sell the stolen jewelry and keep too much of the money," spits Dani.

Caputo is paging through the notebook found in the kitchen. "Very detailed notes in your handwriting. This is the clue we needed. Thank you. Interpol will be interested in what you have here."

Arthur growls, anger flashing in his eyes.

"Okay, Arthur, Dani, and Marco were part of the theft ring. Were there others? John and Linda? Lorenzo?" Karen asks.

"No" comes the swift, defensive response from Lorenzo. His eyes flash angrily.

Caputo holds up his hand. "This is what I know. Those three were involved. John and Linda were victims and easy ones. Dani, while at her pharmacy, learned who was out of town and when, then passed the information to Marco, who did the actual thefts. He gave the stolen items to Arthur. He would find a buyer, sell them, and split the money."

Karen looks at Arthur incredulously. "You stole from friends of yours. That's terrible."

He rolls his eyes. "Yes. Terrible. Linda bragging about the things she has. How they're heirlooms and worth a fortune. It just seemed so right to relieve them of all of it," he states sarcastically.

"But why?" I ask. "You're set to inherit a fortune when your brother dies."

Arthur scoffs. "Well, to be honest, old man, the family wealth is not as large as it once was. My brother's prolonged illness has reduced my inheritance significantly. I'm not getting any younger. I deserve to spend my years living well. It's not like anyone was hurt. Insurance will reimburse everyone," he snarls.

"No one hurt? What about the murders?" Karen asks.

A broad smile crosses Caputo's face. "Marco has a very interesting story to tell about those . . . for a reduction on the theft charges."

Dani jumps out of her chair. An officer places his hand on her shoulder and forces her to sit back down.

"The first to squeal gets the deal." I say.

Caputo arches his eyebrows at me. I wave him off.

Marco relays that Katherine killed Anna. She bought the pins and used the poison dart frog venom that Harriet had ordered from Mario so that Dani could be with Mario. Dani had wanted to kill Katherine because Katherine learned about the thefts, blackmailed her, and planned to use the same poison, but Dani didn't get a chance.

"If Dani didn't kill my daughter, then who did?" Harriet asks. Her eyes grow wide as she realizes the only other person would be Arthur. She turns to face him.

"So sorry, old girl. That stupid cow wanted me out of the way. She was a snoop and found the annual report from the family estate. She planned to take over running the theft ring," Arthur says flatly. "She never realized that I saw her tamper with the electronic cigarette cartridges. She put them in the drawer where I keep my extras, and I knew she had some in her room as well. I just switched out mine for hers. It was only a matter of time before she smoked the wrong one." He put his hands up in surrender.

Harriet releases a gut-wrenching sob. She falls at Arthur's feet, hugging his knees. "No . . . not my daughter. I love you. How could you do this to me?"

"Sorry. She was a bad lot," he replies. "Much like her mother, if you must know. It was merely self-preservation." He shrugs with a smirk on his lips. "Get this woman away from me. She doesn't really love me. It's the idea of being Lady of the Manor she loves. I doubt I would have lasted long after that happened."

An officer assists Harriet back into her chair. She sobs quietly, rocking in place.

Caputo is furiously writing notes. "I will take everyone to the station for formal interviews and to be charged with their crimes."

"Wait!" Karen jumps in. "What about Andrea? Who killed him?" She looks from suspect to suspect. All shake their heads except for Amata.

"Tell us what happened," Caputo pushes. "We recovered the wine bottle and glasses. Your fingerprints were on both, so why throw them in the canal unless you know that traces of poison would be found?"

Amata places her hands over her face. Tears sneak out between her fingers. Softly, her voice starts. "He was not a nice man. She is my friend. We wanted to start again in New York. Divorce would have cost Teresa everything she had worked for. Andrea would not be fair to her. She said she could only be happy if he was dead."

Teresa slaps Amata's face. "I never said that." Her eyes are wild as she looks at each person in the room. "I did want a divorce and for Andrea to buy my part of the restaurant. I was planning to go to New York, but I did not want him dead. I am a great chef and will work hard in a new restaurant."

Amata hangs her head low, deflated. Caputo places his hand under her arm and helps her stand. He and the other officers take Arthur, Dani, Marco, and Amata to the station.

Karen and I watch them trail out of the inn. Harriet decides to also go to the station to be with Arthur. Once Lorenzo and Teresa leave, I lock the front door before trudging up the stairs. Karen is in bed. I remove my shirt and pants, then fall into bed, exhausted.

The next thing I know, my eyes hurt from the bright sunlight streaming into the bedroom. Karen and I get ready and head out of our room to face whatever is downstairs.

I peer over the balcony railing. The hall is immaculate. Food, tables, chairs, and decorations gone. However, Harriet did it, it's amazing.

She walks into the hall. "Oh, good, you're up. I think it would be best for all involved if you left. I'll reimburse you for your stay," she reports coldly.

"Okay. We'll work on finding another place," Karen replies.

Harriet goes on, "Under the circumstances, please make every effort to leave as soon as possible." She huffs. "You've both caused enough damage in this house."

I've had it and snap back at her. "Your husband killed your *daughter* and was part of a theft ring. That wasn't our doing."

"That's not true. He only stated those things because he feared I was part of it. He denies all of it now." She sets her jaw and spits out through gritted teeth, "Please pack your bags and leave!"

"I guess getting breakfast is out of the question!" I yell after her as she heads for the library.

"Come on, Dan. Let's get out of here. She still has the poison dart frog venom in her possession."

How dare she accuse us of being the problem. I'm so angry I could punch a wall. Once we're in our room, Karen begins packing and I use my phone to locate a hotel room within walking distance. Luckily, last night was the end of Carnival. I'm able to secure a room, then I pack my things.

Bags in hand, we head for the new hotel. We're informed that the room won't be ready for several hours, so we leave our luggage at the hotel and wander to the police station. Once there, Caputo greets us at the door. His red eyes have dark bags under them, and stubble covers the lower half of his face. Karen and I complete our witness statements.

Caputo admits that Arthur is now recanting his statement in the library and won't speak without a legal counselor present.

He has been charged with murder and, along with Dani and Marco, his involvement in the theft rings.

"Hey, great luck at being able to find Amata's prints on the wine bottle and glasses. Andrea deserves justice," I say to him.

He smirks. "I lied. The bottle and glasses had little evidence on them. I was sure that either she or Teresa did it."

"Good job! I do feel bad for Amata, though. She'll pay a heavy price for her loyalty." I sigh at the sadness caused and shake my head before collecting my thoughts. "Any idea if Virk played a part in any of it? The murders or the burglaries?"

"Nothing I can find. Teresa did sell the restaurant. She still plans to relocate to New York, but she'll leave Amata behind." He shrugs.

"I know we'll probably need to return to Venice for the trials. I'd like to buy you dinner as a friend." I stand up and shake his hand. Karen gives him a hug.

"I look forward to your return to Venice . . . hopefully without any murders." Caputo winks at us.

Outside, the streets are eerily quiet. Karen and I walk arm in arm along the canal.

"Your thoughts about staying in Italy?" I ask her.

She stops and looks around. "I'm done with Venice for now. I'd like to return someday and actually have a vacation, but there's so much more to Italy. I think we spend the night here and tomorrow continue with the rest of our 'aventure.'"

I agree and snicker to myself. I'm sure Karen has a list of things to see and do, and I can't wait to do them with her.